A V
WHIMSY

'Drenched in irreverence and dripping with wit, *A Whiff of Whimsy* is a medley of amusing meditations on countless facets of life, from the quotidian to the intriguing. Perceptively observing the vagaries of human behaviour, K.C. Verma paints a vibrant portrait of the absurdities that truly make us human, lifting up the ordinary on wings of satire. A skilled storyteller, he deploys the munition of self-deprecatory and whimsical humour to incisive effect. A rollicking triumph!'

—**Shashi Tharoor**
Author and Member of Parliament

'Stephen Leacock, S.J. Perelman, P.G. Wodehouse, James Thurber, Flann O'Brien, Joseph Mitchell—I love each of them dearly, but none has made me laugh as loud, joyfully or as long as K.C. Verma.'

—**Indra Sinha**
Author

'This is delightfully addictive reading. K.C. Verma is clearly India's most enchantingly humorous writer after R.K. Narayan. Gentle, genial, touching.'

—**Philip Mathew**
Editor, *The Week* and *Malayala Manorama*

'Policemen, especially those who have made their way to the top, are normally made of stern, silent stuff, but K.C. Verma is a delightful exception. His earlier books proved his gift for writing and a keen eye for the quirks of ordinary, daily life. This book is no different and is a most enjoyable read.'

—**Ashok Mahadevan**
Former Editor, *Reader's Digest*

A WHIFF OF WHIMSY

K.C. VERMA

RUPA

Published by
Rupa Publications India Pvt. Ltd 2024
7/16, Ansari Road, Daryaganj
New Delhi 110002

Sales centres:
Bengaluru Chennai
Hyderabad Jaipur Kathmandu
Kolkata Mumbai Prayagraj

Copyright © K.C. Verma 2024

This is a work of fiction. Names, characters, places and incidents are either the product of the author's imagination or are used fictitiously and any resemblance to any actual person, living or dead, events or locales is entirely coincidental.

All rights reserved.
No part of this publication may be reproduced, transmitted, or stored in a retrieval system, in any form or by any means, electronic, mechanical, photocopying, recording or otherwise, without the prior permission of the publisher.

P-ISBN: 978-93-6156-329-4
E-ISBN: 978-93-6156-715-5

First impression 2024

10 9 8 7 6 5 4 3 2 1

The moral right of the author has been asserted.

Printed in India

This book is sold subject to the condition that it shall not, by way of trade or otherwise, be lent, resold, hired out, or otherwise circulated, without the publisher's prior consent, in any form of binding or cover other than that in which it is published.

for the little woman

Contents

Once upon a Whim ix

1. Bedroom Shenanigans of the Elderly Kind 1
2. The Monkey's Paw 5
3. Tulsia 12
4. There's a Hole in My Bucket! 17
5. Murder She Said! 21
6. My World Cup Runneth Over 25
7. People Who Live in Glass Houses 32
8. The Banking System and I 37
9. My New Year's Resolution 44
10. Of Granddaughters, Dentures and Creaking Joints . 50
11. The Ultra Man 55
12. Banana Sunday 60
13. The Machines Are Coming! 65
14. The *Sabzimandi* in the Garden of Eden 70
15. Why Me, O Lord! Why Me? 75
16. Selective Amnesia 79
17. Decisions...Decisions! 84
18. Stamp Out the Past 89
19. The Bitter Half 95
20. If Only the Twain Could Meet 101

21.	The Wise Guy	106
22.	And They Lived Happily Ever After	112
23.	Tied in Knots	117
24.	Répondez S'il Vous Plaît	122
25.	A Cool Diwali to All	128
26.	Jugaad: A Point of View	136
27.	*O Tempora! O Mores!*	139
28.	*Qursee Qa Qissa*	144
29.	The Chinwagger Menace	148
30.	Please to Hold	153
31.	Life Goes On	160
32.	*Wah Ustad, Wah!*	168
33.	The Old Is Scared of the Brave New World	171
34.	Three Score Years and Ten	177
35.	The Night of the Meteors (aka You FO)	183
36.	The Poignant Cup	190
37.	Dodos Die Many Deaths	193
38.	*Pakad Lega Polis Wala*	197
39.	Do You Have a Problem?	203
40.	Free Advice	211
41.	Taxing Times	216
42.	*Olloo The Puttar*	224
43.	The Little Woman, the Computer and the Computer Addict	229
44.	The Best Advice I Ever Got	234
45.	The Love Song of King Uncle	238

Once upon a Whim

Why is it that many books carry a preface that is merely a politely worded apology—a sheepish admission of guilt—as if the author has done some dastardly act? The acquirer of the book may or may not learn what unspeakable crime has been committed, but only after they have read the book. An unsolicited disclosure *ab initio* needlessly prejudices the acquirer against the book. A premature confession in the foreword might help the author get something off their chest, but the expiation by the author is hardly fair to the acquirer.

But first, why do I use the term 'acquirer'? Well, anyone who has a book in their possession has quite obviously acquired it; they become readers only once they start reading it. Not all who possess a book have bought it, so not all are buyers. Some may have borrowed it, some may have found it after it had been (deliberately) left behind in an aeroplane, and a few could indeed have stolen it. To refer to the person who has a book in their possession as the acquirer is, therefore, not only correct but accurate.

It is the rights and interests of this hapless acquirer that need to be protected and should certainly take precedence over the urge for catharsis on the part of any author. Instead of an author-centric preface, fairness requires that there be an acquirer-centric approach. It is true that many authors feel the compelling urge to apologize for the stuff they are dishing out, but it is equally true that most acquirers couldn't care less.

They have enough problems of their own, for starters; not all acquirers have a clear idea of what to do with a book once they have acquired one. A preface written with an acquirer-centric approach would serve as a users' manual and advise the acquirer on how best to use the book. After all, if a person has paid good money for it, or has made the effort to borrow or steal one, isn't it the responsibility of the author to ensure that the acquirer derives the maximum benefit from the book?

So, in an unpretentious manner and in simple English, I am giving instructions below in order that any acquirer of this book can efficiently handle their new acquisition.

Step one: Pick up book.
Step two: Open at any page.
Step three: Start reading.
Step four: On reaching the end of a piece, close book.
Step five: Replace book on shelf or bedside table.

Like any other product, this book too comes with a cautionary notice. The whimsy contained in these pages accumulated over a longish period. The happenings have been narrated at different times by a cantankerous old man, by a mildly henpecked husband, by a bemused grandfather, or by a technologically handicapped anachronism caught in a time warp. It is, therefore, likely that rapid readers might get disoriented or confused by the inconsistent mood changes if they read through the book too quickly. Hence it is recommended that not more than a piece or two may be read at one time. For best results, read this book when you have nothing better to do.

(Spoiler alert: The editors would not allow me to use my usual colourful language.)

1
Bedroom Shenanigans of the Elderly Kind

'There it is! There it is!' screamed my wife as she quickly climbed onto the bed.

I too jumped up from my chair and awkwardly clambered onto the writing table. In my hurry, I stepped on the laptop and upended a bottle of ink.

'Where what is?' I asked in a stage whisper, totally mangling the Queen's English.

'The SOB,' said the little woman.

She terms every person, place or thing that annoys her as a SOB, so her clarifying that 'it' was a SOB meant nothing at all. Any husband would be perplexed if the bitter half screams and shouts 'There's the SOB! There's the SOB!'

'Who is the SOB?' I asked patiently, while still perched on the table.

'The liz...the liz...the lizard!' said the wife. By now she was simpering and close to tears. With a trembling finger, she was pointing at a corner of the room.

I followed the line of her arm, from the shoulder to the elbow to the wrist to the shaking finger. And there, in the corner of the room, I saw the littlest gecko, just about an inch long from its bulbous head to its pointy tail. It was so still on the floor that it seemed to be dead.

Although I have not found any scientific proof so far, my theory is that the IQ of geckos decreases with age. That is why when they are young, they roam around on the floor. As they get older, they get stupider and stupider and start climbing walls and hanging upside down from ceilings. But that is only a theory.

'That is a house gecko,' said I pedantically. 'Don't call it a lizard. The term "lizard" is generic in nature and used for many species of reptiles,' I added.

'Oh for God's sake!' shouted my wife. 'Get down from that table, you ridiculous man, and do something about that damn lizard!'

'You mean gecko,' I said under my breath.

Did I tell you that my wife is mortally scared of house geckos, aka lizards?

Well, she is.

'You do understand, my dear, don't you, that this fear that you have is totally irrational?' I asked in the most solicitous tone that I could muster.

'Maybe it's primordial—harking back to the Stone Age and beyond, when a mother's instinct was to protect her brood against the T-Rex and other dangers. You really must overcome this,' said I very reasonably. 'Look at me,' I added. 'I am not scared at all!'

'Yes, I am looking at you, my brave knight! So very brave! Standing there on the table!'

'Oh!' said I.

It struck me that it was possible that I did not present a particularly impressive sight—seventy-odd years of age, corpulent with a noticeable beer belly, perched atop the table with a bottle of ink dripping its contents on the floor, and a possibly damaged computer. I also became conscious of the fact that I was holding a broken pencil in my hand, brandishing it over my head in the same manner that some caveman might wield a club to protect his missus from mastodons, sabre-toothed tigers and assorted baddies.

There must have been some movement in the corner of the room just then because my wife suddenly started screaming again. 'Get down, damn it. Get down! Do something about it. Hit it! Kill it! Get rid of it!'

I lumbered down from the table, taking support of the chair. I gingerly put a foot on the floor, squarely in the middle of a spreading pool of ink. Cautiously, I crept towards the corner where the reptile had last been sighted. But it was nowhere to be seen. Between the zoology lecture and the oh-so-familiar domestic spat, the lizard had made a clean getaway.

'It's gone!' I said triumphantly.

'It's gone,' mimicked the wife, making a moue.

I searched for the offending reptile behind the bookcase, near the wardrobe and along the wall.

Meanwhile, my wife started sniggering.

I turned around and asked, 'Okay, so what's so funny?'

She pointed to the floor, and I jumped. But there was no SOB there. Only the prints of my left foot in blue ink all over the floor. It seemed as if a one-legged drunk had been lurching around the room.

I started giggling. So did my wife. I laughed. She laughed more loudly. We both collapsed in a heap of laughter on the bed. After a while I asked, 'So will you get off the bed at all or not today?'

'Only if you sweep me up in your arms and put me down gently on the floor,' she said.

Did I tell you that my wife is an incorrigible romantic? No? And did I tell you that I know a rather good chiropractor? Well, he says if I rest my back for a couple of months, and if I am lucky, there ought to be no permanent damage!

2

The Monkey's Paw

We have this character—Nawab, who comes around to collect *raddi* (scraps) every Sunday. He is part of that great recycling industry in India that has never even been acknowledged, much less given its due. Nawab will take away anything—old newspapers, plastic wastes, metal scraps, obsolete electronic gadgets and even broken glass. We patronize him because we believe the waste that he takes away will get recycled. And with that small act, we ease our conscience and feel that we have done our bit to save the planet. As a bonus, Nawab also pays us! It may be a trifling amount, but we are only too happy to receive it. We are thankful that the day has not yet come when we need to pay him to take away the rubbish generated by our consumption patterns.

But this story is not about Nawab. It is about a small pocket book that he refused to take with our old newspapers last Sunday. He declared that the pages were too small for making paper bags. 'Moreover, with age, the paper becomes very brittle to be of any use.'

'I wonder what this is,' I said to myself after the *raddiwallah* had left. The book turned out to be the daily astrological horoscope for the year 1967. It contained the annual as well as the day-by-day predictions for all zodiac signs. I have always had a healthy disrespect for such mumbo jumbo, being the rationalist that I am. My wife too is a non-believer, so how a book of astrology could have entered our home was a bit of a mystery.

'Come here, sweetheart,' I called out to my sweetheart in the kitchen. 'I have something to show you!' (When you have been married as long as I have been, you just have to call your wife 'sweetheart'. Believe me, it saves a lot of arguments.)

'Just for the fun of it, let's see what the prediction was for me on this day in 1967,' I said to the little woman. I turned the pages and reached the date.

'Hey! Hey! What the hell is this? My forecast for today in 1967 was "You will reduce your burdens by jettisoning worldly goods that you no longer need. This sacrifice will lead to gain." Oh my gawd! And here I am, selling raddi to Nawab and getting paid for it!'

I looked at the little woman. She looked at me.

'Isn't that creepy?' I asked.

'Oh, that's just a coincidence. Let me see what my forecast was,' said my sweetheart.

'Hah!' She blurted out. 'This is nonsense! It says, "On the farm, you will remain busy with dairy goods and vegetable produce!" That is indeed so funnee! Me? On a farm?' The little woman burst out laughing. Then she stopped all of a sudden. 'Oh my God! Oh my God! Oh my God!'

She read her forecast for the day—of 1967, more than fifty years in the past—once more. This time, she read aloud slowly, 'Farm. Dairy goods? Vegetable produce? Do you...Do you think it could be right?'

I looked at her, quite puzzled.

'Don't you understand?' She almost screamed, as she

dropped the book. 'Dairy goods! Vegetables? I am cooking *matar paneer!* Don't you understand even now?'

If anyone had peeped in through the window, they could have mistaken the little woman and me, frozen in a tableau, for the old couple from the play 'The Monkey's Paw' when they understand that the paw might have supernatural powers. We looked at one another and then fearfully at the book, lying on the floor.

My wife poked it tentatively with her toe. 'It's just a book! Pick it up,' she said.

'You pick it up,' said I.

She cautiously picked it up and replaced it on the bookshelf. 'It is only a coincidence. These things are a load of crap in any case.'

But we were visibly shaken.

The next morning while the little woman was still asleep, I opened the astrology book with morbid fascination to look up my forecast for the day. There was some gobbledygook about my Saturn being in the fifth house of Capricorn which indicated that something sweet would create bitterness.

'Bunkum! Something sweet will create bitterness. Bah!' I said to myself and went to the kitchen to make tea. As I poured the hot water, I accidentally knocked over the pot of sugar and it smashed on the floor. In a flash, I understood. The little woman would definitely be annoyed with me for breaking the pot and wasting sugar. Something sweet would certainly create bitterness!

Because of this experience, on Tuesday, I thought it would be prudent to check my horoscope for the day. The book was not where I had left it but on the countertop in the kitchen. Obviously, the little woman had been reading it too.

I was relieved to find that it prophesied something totally implausible: 'You will discover buried treasure today.'

The day passed uneventfully enough, but I was in for a shock in the evening. When I was changing my shoes, I noticed something shiny under the shoe rack. It turned out to be a five-rupee coin! 'Would it qualify as buried treasure?' I wondered.

The day after, I looked for it but the book was nowhere to be seen. Ultimately, I found it near the washing machine. I had no option but to confront the little woman. Sheepishly, she admitted that she had been consulting the pocket book every day.

'But it is nonsense!' I said, cleverly deflecting any suspicion she might have had about my consulting it too.

'Do you really think I don't know that you too have been reading the book every day?' she asked. 'But it does have something in it, doesn't it? On Monday, my horoscope said I should drive carefully in order to avoid any accidents, and guess what? I did drive carefully and there was no accident! Then yesterday, the horoscope said that I would meet an old friend, and I ran into Pinky at the post office.'

'But sweetheart, Pinky lives next door!'

'I know, but she is also an old friend, isn't she? And do you know what the forecast for today was? It said that something that I want to keep hidden will get exposed and cause embarrassment. And you have caught me! But you must read the portion related to personality traits. It's so, so accurate!'

She started riffling through the pages. 'Here it is! "Personality Traits"! About you it says: "You are gullible but not easy to fool. You are kind, generous, broadminded, tolerant, considerate, friendly, warm-hearted and sincere. You are predisposed to go to extreme lengths to impress members of the opposite sex."'

She looked at me accusingly and said, 'See?'

Very much like all our conversations these days, she had latched on to just that one sentence, and started belabouring me with it, totally disregarding the bigger picture. All my good qualities amounted to nothing, even though certified by no less an authority than the horoscope of 1967.

'Here, give me that,' I said, and started going through the book, till I found the zodiac sign of the little woman. The planetary position was explained in complicated jargon—something about Venus, Rahu, Ketu, Leo, occlusions, transits, houses, ascendants and stuff.

The personality traits listed for my sweetheart's zodiac sign were a masterpiece of creative writing. Even though she might have hidden her qualities under a bushel or two, that book made me rediscover the little woman. It said she was hardworking, kind-hearted, had a positive attitude, a cheerful disposition, was a good manager and thrifty to boot—all very praiseworthy qualities indeed! Any husband would be delighted to discover these in his wife. But this is not what I needed. I wanted something damning and I needed it quickly, otherwise she would never stop badgering me about my predisposition 'to go to extreme lengths to impress members of the opposite sex'.

Just as I was despairing, a small sentence caught my eye. 'Aha!' I said. 'Listen to what it says about you and your qualities of heart and mind, sweetheart. Listen carefully. It says, "Your habit of secretly stashing money away, without telling the spouse, will lead to domestic discord."'

'I am sorry,' the little woman blanched. 'I promise I won't

do it in future. But you too must promise that you won't keep trying to impress girls.'

'Bingo!' I thought to myself. The shot in the dark had hit the bullseye! Even while this thought crossed my mind, I felt the book jump in my hand, as if it were a little monkey's paw.

Our quarrel continued until late that night, steeped in mutual distrust as we were, according to the 'future' as foretold for both of us in the past. Predictions made when we were yet to marry. Predictions that were not predictions at all; but which seemed to be coming true in an uncanny manner. At the end, to find some remedy, we turned to that same book with its eclipses of Mars, occlusions of Jupiter, and transitions through the cusp of Leo and Aquarius.

There, under the heading 'Forecast for Married Life', we found that the stars foretold in 1967 that the little woman would marry a person with 'little or no belief in astrology!' The advice for me was that if I wanted a happy marriage, I should not allow the stars and planets to rule my life.

We went to bed very late but with a clear resolve. This morning, we drove to the bridge over the Yamuna River and stopped right in the middle. Both of us got out, and together, we ceremoniously dumped that evil book into the swirling waters below. We returned home, joking and laughing together; something which we had not done for the past many days.

The newspaper was lying on the doorstep, where the newsboy usually throws it. Just to underline our breaking free from that hocus-pocus of horoscopes, I said to my wife, 'Let's see what the stars foretell for me today.' As I turned to the horoscope section of the paper, we both giggled like little children stealing some forbidden fruit.

Our giggling stopped when I read aloud my horoscope for the day.

'You will rid yourself of some malignant influence today.'

'Oh damn,' I whispered. 'Not again!'

3
Tulsia

Everyone's childhood is populated by strange uncles, a few ghosts and other weirdos like that mysterious cousin who always arrives from somewhere in the middle of the night and is gone by the morning. I, too, have had my share of characters, including the witch that lived under the tamarind tree that we had to pass whenever we went to the market. I well remember Kalimdad Khan, our gardener, and Man Bahadur Thapa, one of the orderlies who always begged me to knock off a crow with my air gun. And Phulo. And Chunnu Mian. And Ganeshi.

And then there was Tulsia.

Tulsia's exact status in the household remained unclear to me. He was treated as an advisor, but he was also undoubtedly a servant. He washed clothes, cleaned the utensils and drew water from the well. But then there were times when he did not.

He behaved as if he was the majority shareholder of a proprietary company and it was for the minority shareholders—all members of the family—to kowtow to him. He treated the family as his own and indiscriminately upbraided all the servants, as well as my mother, my aunt and any other member of the family who he felt was not performing up to the standards expected by him.

The only two who he dared not admonish were my grandmother and my father.

At all times, it was exasperating to tell him anything because he was hard of hearing. Often, even after shouting in his ear, it was impossible to make him understand what one wanted him to do. But, quite miraculously, he heard anything about food that might be said even softly behind his back.

With an unspecified charter and a mulish obstinacy to do as he pleased, Tulsia was a nuisance in the home that I grew up in. One never knew what he might (or might not) do. It was not that he did not work. In fact, life would have been much easier if he worked less.

Without asking anyone he would wash the clothes that needed to be washed, and even those that did not. He washed my school blazer and wrung the life out of it, claiming that it had seemed a bit soiled. Once when my father was expecting important guests for evening tea, Tulsia took down the curtains of the drawing room and proceeded to soak them for a wash. Mother discovered what had happened just an hour before the guests were to arrive. The wet curtains were hung in place and we were given strict instructions not to peek from behind them, as we usually did when there were grown-up visitors.

Another time, Tulsia uprooted all the rose bushes and planted vegetable seeds. 'We don't eat roses! We eat spinach!' he said. As far as I recall, no roses or any spinach ever grew again in that particular patch of the garden.

But of the duties that Tulsia took upon himself, the one which he took most seriously was to keep us—the children—amused. He introduced us to impossible games. I learnt a peculiar version of rock-paper-scissors which required the use of both hands. The passing years have dimmed the rules, which is just as well. Even as the contours of the game escape my memory, I recall it was heaps of fun. It definitely involved a lot of laughter. I do not think today I would be able to get my grandchildren to play that game, even if I were to invent the missing pieces of the rules. Suffice it to say that it was an extremely complicated version of rock-paper-scissors-lizard-Spock.

Tulsia was good at shooting marbles. He taught us how to fly kites. He could spin a top by throwing it in the air and then deftly making it land on his palm, spinning all the while. He could make a yo-yo out of empty boot polish containers.

But Tulsia's favourite game was an amalgam of Chinese checkers and draughts, played on an hourglass-shaped grid that could be drawn in the dust or marked on any hard surface. We would play the game endlessly, but Tulsia was the permanent champion. Sometimes the grid was drawn on cardboard with a piece of chalk, while at other times it was scratched on the floor with a piece of coal. The 'draughtsmen' were usually pebbles, nine to a player. Once in a while, the game was played with paisa or *anna* coins. When we used coins as draughtsmen, the game was played secretively because it was akin to gambling. The victor of any game won all coins on the board! While I remember that Tulsia always won, I do not remember him ever having pocketed any coins. Maybe he never played for money against us.

Tulsia also kept us beguiled with his stories. He told us stories from mythology and history, from mountains and faraway lands. But we best liked the stories which he made up for us. Depending on his mood, he would narrate tales of cobblers and kings, of fairies and Angrezi *mem*s, of fire-breathing dragons and djinns. In his different stories, he was often a thief, a brigand or a murderer. Though we knew it was all made up, we still got goose pimples when he spoke in the baritone of *Dakoo* Tulsi Thakur.

He would alternatively claim that he had run away from a quarrelsome wife, escaped after murdering a moneylender in his village, or lost his parents after being kidnapped as a child. He led us to believe that he was wanted by the police in many states—for cheating, for theft and for murder. Probably to lend credence to such stories, he would disappear from home from time to time. He would reappear suddenly, after some days or a few months, with no explanation whatsoever for his absence. He would then proceed to take charge of the household as if he had never been away.

Then, one day, he went away and did not return. Months passed, then a year, and another. We gave up any hope of his ever returning. Then, almost three years later, an unkempt figure in saffron robes arrived at our doorstep. Tulsia claimed that he had been living as a hermit in the Himalayas. He said he had seen a bright light in a dream, which taught him how to fly and how to live for a thousand years.

With his long-matted locks and flowing black beard, Tulsia then established himself firmly in the veranda. Whether sitting or lying down, he would mumble nonsensical rhymes all day long. He steadfastly refused to do any work, demanding to be fed at regular hours since he was now an enlightened *sanyasi*. My aunt found his behaviour absolutely unacceptable, especially because he kept insisting that he would stay for a thousand years. She bluntly suggested more than once that Tulsia should go back to the Himalayas, but he refused to oblige her.

Then, one day, he disappeared again. As usual, he did not reveal to anyone that he would go away. The only difference was that this time he did not return. Now I shall never know whether he had murdered the moneylender or run away from a nagging wife. Or even if he had ever had a wife at all.

Considering that Tulsia was about seventy when he last disappeared and that more than fifty years have passed since then, it's unlikely that Tulsia is still alive. But suppose he was telling the truth about having learnt how to live for a thousand years? Would I be surprised if a one-hundred-and-twenty-year-old Tulsia walked into my home today, mumbling some nonsensical rhyme?

4
There's a Hole in My Bucket!

'Pshaw! This is hogwash!' exclaimed Guddan, my twelve-year-old granddaughter.

'Language, lady! Language!' I warned, without taking my eyes off the television.

'But you use words like bullshit all the time, Nana!' she protested. 'Whether you agree or not, this lesson here is all BS—as you would say.'

I turned away from the television to look at what she was doing. It seemed to be her homework.

'What is it?'

'It's maths. I hate maths!' she declared with finality.

This is the same girl who had complained in class two that she was no longer interested in studying maths because she had learned all that there was to be learnt.

'They are making us do the same stuff,' she had complained.

'What same stuff?' I had asked quite unsuspectingly.

'Addition!' She had said. 'We have already learnt addition last year in class one, and again our teacher wants us to add numbers. I am in a new class and they should teach something new. But the teacher says we still have to add, even when we do multi-pilkashun. She says we will have to use addition throughout our lives! What's the point of learning something in one class if you have to learn it again in the next?'

Starting as that maths prodigy, she has only lived up to the promise of those early days. I am all too aware that now she constantly finds fault with the education system, her school, her teachers, the books, the questions, and even the answers to those questions at the end of the book.

'What seems to be the problem this time?' I asked in an effort to discover what it was that had forced my not-so-well-behaved granddaughter to use strong language.

'It's all so stupid, Nana. Why should I find the time taken to fill water in a bucket if it flows in through two taps and at the same time drains out through a hole in its bottom? What kind of a stupid person would do that? He should first plug the hole and then fill water.'

I fully empathized with her and saw the logic of her arguments. When we were kids, two demented characters called Mr Hall and Mr Knight used to ask us a large number of such similar questions with no method to the madness—water flowing in, water flowing out, big taps, small taps, tanks with leaks, buckets with holes, tubs with missing stoppers, swimming pools with drainpipes, barrels without spigots and drums without plugs!

Apparently, those holes that were there in buckets when we were children have not been fixed even after sixty years. Water was being wasted then and even now! We boast of being such a wonderful country, and yet we have been unable to fix a hole in a bucket?

When our generation was confronted with the grim issue of water wastage in this manner, we did wonder what kind of foolishness it was. But while we wondered, we never dared question the wisdom of the omnipotent Mr Hall and Mr Knight, and the assorted fillers of leaky tubs and holey buckets.

But now it is a brave new world! The children of today are far more aware and will not tolerate wastage, even if it is in the pages of their textbooks.

'Why aren't maths teachers more aware of the environment?' demanded Guddan. 'Why don't they fix the leak or turn that tap off?'

Even as I struggled to find an answer, she took up another peeve. 'Why do we have to learn tables? And that too up to twenty times twenty?'

I mumbled something about equipping children to perform mental maths operations and be capable of quickly multiplying numbers.

'That's what calculators are for, Nana! Why can't we use calculators? If you won't allow children to use things like calculators, why do people go around inventing them in the first place?'

I could quite see her point. A valid point. When we were young, we did not dare ask such questions, and when we finally moved on from tables for long multiplication, we fell into a maelstrom of log tables, slide rules and gear-operated Facit machines. I did not have the heart to tell Guddan that she was better off with multiplication tables.

'Tables suck!'

In passing, I made a mental note that while the reasons for exasperation do not change, vocabulary does. I remembered that the phrase used most often by Guddan's mother was 'It stinks!' I was still trying to recall which word had been our favourite when Guddan launched a veritable broadside against maths.

'Why can't people constructing walls get the right kind of workmen? Why do I have to calculate how long it will take to build a wall if half the workers run away after three days?'

I had no answer for that. I looked at her but there was something in that combative look which warned me against increasing her store of trivia by talking about Nawab Asaf-ud-Daula and the Imambaras that he got built in Lucknow.

Guddan bashed on. 'Nana, have you ever seen a garden in the shape of a rhombus? Have you ever wondered why anyone would want to make a two-metre-wide path through it? Why is it that all lawns in maths books are perfect circles? Have you ever seen me wear any ribbons, and that too metres of that stuff? And Nana, what's lace? My maths book talks about stitching laces on handkerchiefs, pillows, tablecloths and even curtains. And what does stitching mean? Why can't parallel lines meet?'

'You see, dear Guddan, it is like th...'

Guddan was in full flow. She ploughed ahead. 'Why is there a hippopotamus in a triangle? Why don't A and B have proper names? Why is diameter not spelt the same way as a metre?'

'Listen to me, Guddan, when I was...'

But she interrupted me again to deliver the coup de grâce, 'And why are fractions vulgar?'

'Look, I don't know, and I don't care. Why don't you do me a favour...,' I said in frustration, '...go and ask Nani. She knows the answer to every question. Go!'

Guddan went and I heard her say something to her Nani in the kitchen. Then I heard Nani say loudly, 'Oh, yeah! Nana said so, did he?'

I then heard Nani use pretty strong language in praise of Nana. So before Guddan could return from the kitchen, I made good my escape to the club.

5
Murder She Said!

'I am sure they have a dead body in that suitcase,' said my wife.

We watched the coolie struggle to stow the bulky piece of baggage in the overhead rack.

'No. I think they are eloping. The suitcase contains family jewels. That's why it's so heavy.'

The man paid the coolie. 'Did you see that? Did you see that! He paid the coolie a hundred rupees! He paid so much only because there's a body in there.'

'No. No. No.' I said softly so as not to be overheard. 'They are certainly running away from home. This is a Heer–Ranjha case!'

'But Heer and Ranjha never ran away together.'

'Does it matter? Won't you recognize Romeo and Juliet when you see them?'

'Oh, shut up!'

Train journeys can be fairly boring for elderly couples like us, who frequently travel between Chandigarh and Delhi. To pass the time, my wife and I play this little game. We build stories around our co-passengers, try to guess their professions, and speculate on the reason for their journey. We talk softly, of course. It would be embarrassing indeed if others heard the wild ideas that my wife comes up with.

The Shatabdi is such a convenient train. Two tickets from Chandigarh to Delhi cost just about a thousand rupees for senior citizens. The chair car seating also provides a modicum of privacy, with an aisle separating the two pairs of seats. The seats in the middle of each coach are placed such that two rows of passengers face each other. Heer and Ranjha seated themselves across the aisle from our seats.

'They don't seem to be married. Heer is not wearing any *sindoor*. See?'

'Sindoor ruins the hair. You also don't use any vermillion, do you? That doesn't mean we are not married to each other.'

'Oh, if only!' she sighed.

'What did you say?'

'Nothing. Nothing at all,' she muttered.

'Look at Heer and Ranjha,' said I. 'They seem to be highly amused about something. Heer is giggling. Such a loving couple! They are holding hands.'

'What is romantic about holding hands?' asked my wife, petulantly. 'Did you notice that her hands are moving constantly? He is holding her hands to stop them from shaking. Anyone would be nervous if they were carrying a body in their luggage.' My wife said this with all the confidence of a seasoned carrier of dead bodies in suitcases.

'Watch very carefully. I think there is something dripping from their suitcase. Could it be blood?'

'Shush...' said I, somewhat loudly.

'If there's no blood, it's bound to be drugs.'

'Don't be silly, dear. They are such an innocent-looking couple,' said I.

'You are always so gullible. Of course they are an innocent-looking couple! Do you think the South American drug mafia would employ anyone looking like a thug?'

Heer and Ranjha looked at us from across the aisle. They smiled. I smiled back. I could only hope that the clattering of the train was drowning my wife's voice. Heer's fingers did a quick dance and Ranjha took both her hands in his and smiled. She seemed to giggle.

The little woman reconsidered her verdict after a short while. 'No! I don't think it is drugs. It is murder. For all you know, this might not be the first murder that your innocent-looking couple has committed.'

For the rest of the journey, my wife embroidered her story further: An inconvenient lover. Blackmail. A murder. A body to be disposed of. Several murders, committed in different places. Many bodies disposed of at random in trains.

I was equally vehement that Heer and Ranjha would get married in some temple in Delhi the next morning.

By and by, the Shatabdi came to a halt at New Delhi railway station and the train emptied quickly. A couple of coolies entered our coach, looking for heavy pieces of baggage that the owners might need help with. Ranjha gestured to a coolie to unload their suitcase.

As we started to get out, Ranjha turned to us. 'Hats off to you, sir and madam,' said he, with a wink. 'You have the most fertile imagination. But we are sorry to disappoint you. We are both married. To each other. For the past five years. The suitcase contains books, which is why it is so heavy.'

He added, 'By a strange coincidence, my wife's name is indeed Heer.'

We both must have looked astonished because his wife explained, 'Both of us teach sign language and lip reading to hearing-impaired children. On train journeys, we pass the time by eavesdropping, so to say, on conversations of fellow passengers. We have never enjoyed a train journey as much as we did today! Thank you.'

One hundred rupees for the coolie. A thousand rupees for two tickets to Delhi. The sheepish look on our faces? Priceless!

6
My World Cup Runneth Over

Who from amongst us has never been a Boy Scout? And can any of us ever forget the injunction given to us by Lord Baden-Powell?

'Be Prepared!'

Yes! Always be prepared. Thus, in the last week of May, I made a few trips to the neighbourhood *Angrezi Sharab ki Dukan* and bought substantial quantities of beer. Also, four bottles of vodka. And one bottle of gin. And a couple of bottles of whisky. Just to be on the safe side, you understand? After all, one has to be prepared.

'Are we expecting guests?' asked the missus, my better half for more than forty years.

'No. No, I am only stocking up for the World Cup. In all, about fifty matches will be played till the end of June. If I have to watch them all, I will need lots of beer. And who knows, if the boys in blue do well, I might even need to open that bottle of Dom which I have been saving for an appropriate occasion.'

Then I stationed myself before the television set, with two cans of chilled beer. 'What does beer have to do with cricket?' asked the little woman in her usual acerbic tone.

'Well,' said I in a slow drawl while taking a sip from a freshly opened can, 'It is a very complicated thing. You won't understand it.'

'Try me!' she said. Petulantly.

With great presence of mind, I spilt some beer on the TV remote and escaped from the room on the pretext of drying it.

The very next day, when a match had just started, we had a disagreement of sorts. 'You mean to say that you will watch television every day from one thirty till ten at night?'

'That's right,' said I. 'And on some days, when there are two matches, I might watch till longer.'

'What about my serials?' she wailed. Then she mumbled something rude, which I could not quite make out. I did not consider it prudent to ask her to repeat what she had said.

Now my wife has many qualities and I never tire of praising her, but patience is simply not one of her virtues. Take for instance the day when the match was delayed because of rain. I stationed myself and my beer in front of the TV and kept waiting for the rain to stop. In the interregnum, I enlarged my knowledge of the game by closely following the different discussions on various TV channels. Each time they showed the pitch with the covers and the wet outfield, I opened a fresh can of beer. But was the missus so patient?

Oh no, not at all. She kept insisting that I should switch channels to some stupid drama serial that she was following. I had to keep reassuring her that even though there was no likelihood of play, one could not take a chance. Be prepared and all that, you know! In her predictable fashion, she stomped out of the room.

She peeped in an hour later. On TV, three experts were discussing the game.

'What? Is it raining still?'

'No, dear. The match has been abandoned. But they are talking about it.'

'Well...They have been doing that for the past three hours. I am beginning to think that this cricket is more talk than play.'

'Oh no! Cricket is a serious matter. It is the game that counts and nothing else,' I countered.

'I understand that. In our kitty parties, we play gin rummy seriously. It's the rummy that counts. We play. We talk. We play a bit more. Then we talk. And then we talk a bit more. Yeah. I get it. Cricket is serious stuff.'

Before I could think of a scathing riposte, she flounced out of the room.

We did not talk to each other for the rest of the evening. Or the next day either.

So when India had to play that important match last week, I thought I would enlist her support right from the beginning. This was in keeping with my general philosophy of adopting the path of least resistance and the teachings of the Buddha to adopt the middle path.

'Why don't you sit with me for some time and maybe then I will be able to explain the finer points of the game to you?'

'But you said it was a complicated thing and I wouldn't understand it.'

'Doesn't matter,' I said. 'You must try. Okay?' And I proceeded to give a short introductory lecture on the basics of powerplay, bouncers and the thirty-yard circle.

She protested mildly. 'I already know all that,' she claimed. 'I also recognize Gavaskar, Pataudi and Tendulkar. I also know Shastri, Kumble and Dhoni. In any case, I expect your cricket to be boring, so I shall read this magazine.'

I told her that cricket can never be boring and that it

was India that was playing. She clearly did not share my enthusiasm and was a bit disappointed for not finding any familiar faces.

A little later, she looked at the screen again. 'Isn't that Dhoni?' she asked.

'Yes, it is,' I confirmed.

'Then what is he doing playing kabaddi? Wasn't he standing there with all those pads and stuff?'

'That is an ad for the kabaddi league,' I said, exasperated. It is really so irritating having to explain everything.

'Then they should find some kabaddi player to advertise the kabaddi league,' she said petulantly. 'It's so confusing.'

'And what's this big deal about his gloves?' she asked a bit later.

'It is a very complicated thing. Don't let the details bother you, my dear,' I said. 'It is a matter of national pride!'

'That means you don't know what it is about, isn't that so?'

'Oh, don't be silly! It is a matter of national pride. Everything about our cricket team is a matter of national pride.'

Suddenly she shouted, 'Oh look! Look! It is Anushka's husband!'

I looked around the room. I craned my neck and peeped into the other room. I could see no one.

'I see no one. Where is this guy? And who is Anushka?'

It took me a while to understand that my wife was talking about Virat Kohli. I also got to know who Anushka was, though now I am not so certain what she does.

'Why is our team sponsored by Oppo? Isn't that a Chinese firm? Aren't there any Indian companies willing to sponsor our team?'

'What difference does it make, my dear? Oppo must have

offered the highest amount!'

'But you said it is a matter of national pride, no?'

'It is a very complicated thing. You won't understand it.'

'Try me!' she said. Belligerently.

'Let me watch the game I say,' said I.

She kept quiet, but only for some time. She spoke up when about thirty overs had been bowled. She enquired sweetly, 'Darling, who is winning?'

I frowned and managed to keep a straight face.

Five or six overs later, she again asked, 'Darling, who is winning now?'

This time, I almost exploded. I left the room, went to the loo, got a fresh can of beer and returned only when I had calmed down.

'How does this Duckling Woodchuck thing work?' She asked, apropos of nothing.

'The what? Oh! I think you mean the Duckworth Lewis System. Darling, the DLS is a very complicated thing. You won't understand it.'

'Try me!' she said. Testily.

'Oh, look at that shot!' I squealed excitedly, pointing at the TV.

'So, you are saying that the DLS or whatever is complicated. What about this DRS thing?'

'The DRS? Oh, you mean the DRS! The DRS is also a very complicated thing. You won't understand it.'

'Try me!' she said. Combatively.

'Let me get another beer,' I said and went to the fridge, and returned after a longish while.

Finally, we were able to sit together companionably and watch the match. I let out whoops of joy or groans of disappointment as the game progressed. The dear wife followed suit, and started quite enjoying herself. She even managed a wolf-whistle once, something that I had never been able to do.

'Oh goody! He has hit a sixer!' She shouted.

'Oh goody! He has hit a sixer again!'

'Oh goody! He has hit a sixer yet again!'

'Listen darling, that was one six. The rest were replays. Cricket was always a spectators' game but now it is a TV game...'

But she interrupted me: 'Look! Look! He has hit a sixer again! This is a different sixer because the boundary looks different.'

'It looks different because that is a replay of a similar six that this batsman had hit in the last World Cup. Didn't you see that the batsman and the fielder were wearing different uniforms?'

'Oh? Why can't they show the game that is in progress? They show Tendulkar sitting with that funny-looking mike. Gavaskar is not even playing. They show Anushka's husband selling Vicks *ki goli*. You point to some bald man and say that is Sehwag. There are a whole lot of new faces and names. What the heck! This is all too confusing.

'I give up,' she said decisively. 'I will never understand this game.'

'But that is what I said darling, it's a very complicated thing. You won't understand it.'

And I heaved a sigh of relief. Now there would only be me, my beer, my TV and my World Cup. Aah!

But I was wrong.

She snatched the remote from my hand and switched to her favourite soap channel.

For the last three matches, I have been sitting by my wife every evening, watching one meaningless serial after another. If I request her politely enough, she sometimes lets me switch to a sports channel to know the score. And then again, sometimes she does not.

Married life is a very complicated thing. I do not think I will ever understand it.

7
People Who Live in Glass Houses

There I was, sitting peacefully in the garden, minding my own business. But is anyone ever allowed to sit peacefully? No! This time it was Pandeyji, who came rushing to me, all in a tizzy.

'They've found me out! They've found me out! Now I know they've been keeping me under watch! Oh, what shall I do? You must help me. I haven't been able to sleep all night!'

'Hey! Hey! Hold your horses,' said I. 'What's your problem?'

'Don't you read the papers? The Chinese are coming! They have been monitoring my phone, my computer, my Facebook, my Twitter account and Instagram. Oh my God! I feel so violated.'

I was more annoyed than puzzled. In our colony, Pandeyji is the resident paranoid. He can be trusted to squeeze drama out of even a mosquito bite. Besides being a raving hypochondriac, he also has extreme notions of self-importance.

'Don't you understand? This SheeJingPing chap has gotten all the data on me. National security is now in great danger! The newspapers say that the Chinks have kept ten thousand people under surveillance in India. You know, the President, the ministers, the captains of industry and senior officers! Surely, I must be among the most senior. There aren't so many officers, as you well know.'

Quite heartlessly I said, 'Don't worry, the Chinese have better things to do. And I am sure they have more important people to snoop on.'

For those who have not met Pandeyji, I need to explain that he is the only one in our colony of former civil servants who retired as an 'officer'. You see, most of us served this *sarkar* or that, and we had designations like secretary or additional secretary or joint secretary. It was only Pandeyji who had the designation of OSD or Officer on Special Duty. Not inaccurately, Pandeyji believes that he was the only 'officer', while the rest of us were mere secretaries, the likes of which you would find under this rock and that.

The fact that Pandeyji was Officer on Special Duty in the Centre for Overseeing the Working of the Department of Untreated Natural Garbage does not faze him one bit. In fact, he is rather proud of his organization.

'There may not be many officers, Pandeyji, but you retired more than ten years back, didn't you? And that too from a department which was a hybrid of animal husbandry and sanitation. What secrets can you reveal that might endanger our country?'

'That's just it! I can't tell you, can I? I was privy to so much sensitive information. You can't imagine the amount of natural garbage we used to dispose of. Especially from around the different ministries and Raisina Hill. The Chinks would be interested in that. Moreover, I don't like chow mein. That SheeJingPing character might have an additional grouse against me for this reason.'

'Pandeyji, you also don't eat beef, so the Americans too could be out to get you,' I suggested mischievously.

'No, no! The Americans won't do anything against me, because I love hotdogs. But I am really worried about the Chinks.'

'Relax, Pandeyji. You have nothing to worry about. Neither the Chinese nor the Americans would have the inclination or the need to bother about retired officers.' I said this partly to reassure Pandeyji and partly to get rid of him.

'The government has appointed a committee to look into this matter. Do you think I should...' he said uncertainly.

I could make out that he was torn between two powerful emotions. One was the comfort of anonymous security, accepting that he did not figure among the VIPs. The other was that terrible fear of being spied on by enemies, named and unnamed. One was shameful obscurity, the other a delicious nightmare of hauteur.

Hubris won.

'No! I think I will report my suspicions to the government,' he declared.

'Look Pandeyji,' I reasoned, 'Why are you worried? Everyone collects data. Every server has backdoors. Every phone is probably tapped. All metadata is analysed. And all countries do it. Maybe even Vanuatu has been targeting the USA and China.'

'Who is Mr Vannoo Attoo?'

'Forget that, Pandeyji. What I mean to say is that even our neighbourhood stores spy on you. You provide your cell phone number to the *lala* for loyalty points each time you shop there, don't you?'

'Of course I do! The lala is not a Chinky! Or haven't you noticed?'

'Well, I am sure that even our lala sells the information about our purchases to market researchers, who determine the consumption patterns in our colony. You should just count yourself lucky if information regarding your cereal preference is not sold to a rival manufacturer so that they can target you in their next advertising campaign.'

That stopped Pandeyji in his tracks. In his Centre for Overseeing the Working of the Department of Untreated Natural Garbage, he had never applied his mind to such issues.

'You mean the lala as well as the Chinese know everything about me!' he wailed.

'How much they know is directly proportional to your stupidity. It depends on how carelessly you use your phone and computer, and sometimes you don't even have to use it. For example, I am sure Sundar Pichai knows more about you than the Chinese do. Here, let me show you. Give me your phone,' I said and extended my hand.

Then I showed the OSD of the Centre for Overseeing yada yada yada the journal entries in his fitness app. 'See here,' I said, 'This shows all the places you visited in the past many days. It also shows that last Thursday you walked to the sector market. Did you go to the liquor shop?'

'Shh, don't say that loudly! And definitely never tell your *bhabiji!*'

My bhabiji? I wondered. Why would I tell my bhabiji? My brother and bhabi live nearby, but why on earth would I mention to my brother or his wife that Pandeyji had gone to the liquor shop? It took a while for me to understand that Pandeyji meant that I must not tell his wife.

'But Mark Zuckerberg and Jeff Bezos and Jan Koum and probably even Jack Ma know that you went to the liquor shop,' I said teasingly.

'Who are all these people? And don't they have anything better to do?' asked Pandeyji.

'Precisely! So while the Chinese can indeed deduce much from your phone and other electronic records, the question is—would they want to?'

Pandeyji considered this to be an insult to his very being, his pride in being the only officer among mere secretaries. I could almost see the dawning realization in his eyes that his thirty-five years in the Centre for Overseeing the Working of the Department of Untreated Natural Garbage amounted to little more than the acronym of his centre.

'And all those important matters I handled...' His voice petered out. 'So how much do the Chinese actually know?'

I thought for some time. Then I gave him the most honest answer that I could. 'How much do the Chinese know? Maybe as much as the Americans. And the Israelis. And the Portuguese. And the Russians. And the French. And the Angolans. And the Brazilians. And the Vanuatuans...

'So, Pandeyji, now do you understand?'

'Yes,' said Pandeyji. With rare insight, he summed up our discussion. 'Yes, I understand. People who live in glass houses should not change clothes!'

8
The Banking System and I

Have you heard of that French Sheikh, Pierre, who has said so many clever things? One of them is something about the good that men do being forgotten over the years, while the evil haunts them for long and makes them lose sleep. And so has it been with me! In these times of direct enforcement by the Enforcement Directorate and investigations by the Central Bureau of Investigation and failing banks and assorted skeletons tumbling out of bank lockers, I can only pray that Sheikh Pierre was mistaken.

You see, I lose sleep! I lose sleep because I was the pioneer of manipulating the banking system while appearing to adhere to every rule, regulation and practice. It was in the mid-1960s that I had hoodwinked the system and used it for personal gain. I live in fear that my crime might get detected now!

You would understand better if I were to tell you that I had indeed asked the beauty queen of our class out for a cup of coffee. Not once, but many times. And she always declined. It could not really be said that she ever refused. She never refused. But sometimes it was this and sometimes that. The word 'declined', therefore, summed it up neatly. It also left me with a sliver of hope—a hope that one day the prettiest girl in the class would agree to let me take her out to the Coffee House.

And indeed, one day she came up to me and said, 'Let's go to the Coffee House today. I'll meet you there at one.'

It was said pleasantly enough. It was not said as a request. It was not said as an order. It was said exactly as a queen might carelessly bestow a minor favour—'Minion, we permit you to take us to the Coffee House today.'

But the gods can be cruel indeed, and maybe a little jealous too! That day, I had only one rupee in my pocket. On some days, I did have more money, but a single rupee was the absolute rock bottom! One rupee was just enough to look after my needs for the day. My budgeting at 1966 prices was precise: twenty-four paisa for a cup of coffee, thirty-seven paisa for lunch consisting of a masala dosa, and thirty-five paisa for the bus ride home. This financial outlay left a generous tip of four paisa for Sher Singh, the head waiter of the Coffee House. Beauty queen agreeing to accompany me to the Coffee House that day, therefore, constituted a financial crisis of epic proportions. After all, from where was I to mobilize the additional revenue? All my friends, like me, constantly flirted with the poverty line.

In between the morning lectures, I begged Tomar, Dixit and Hari to lend me a few rupees. Between the three of them, they could cough up just one rupee and fifty paisa. They stipulated that I repay the loan within two days and, by way of interest, I was to give them a full account of my tryst.

With two rupees and fifty paisa in my pocket, I felt more confident; almost safe. Apart from the standard fare of masala dosa and coffee, the only other good offering on the menu of the Coffee House was fruit jelly with fresh cream, and that cost a whole rupee! So even if she ordered a dosa, a fruit jelly and both of us had coffee, my financial situation would remain satisfactory. Maybe I could even give a huge tip of ten paisa to Sher Singh in order to make a good impression!

But what if she ordered cold coffee, which cost sixty-two paisa? Then I would have no option but to make some excuse and not have any coffee myself. Or sacrifice the bus fare and walk home!

I skipped the last lecture before the lunch break in order to grab a table at the Coffee House, which usually got crowded at lunch. I looked around. All tables were full. And glory be! There was not a single familiar face in sight! When someone meets a girl in a coffee house, the last thing they want is sundry acquaintances sniggering, ogling and drooling!

I kept looking at the door and soon enough, she came. But wait! Why did she have her friend in tow? I was disappointed to find that she, to whom I had planned to say so many sweet nothings, had come with a personal chaperone. But the disappointment of not being able to murmur endearments was a minor concern. The major concern was the possibility that the chaperone might also want a dosa and a coffee!

We settled down and I asked the ladies what they would like. The beauty queen demurely asked for a dosa and coffee, but the chaperone wanted a dosa, a fruit jelly and a cold coffee! Sher Singh took the order, and I followed him to the kitchen. I told him in a soft voice to delay the order and also asked him if he would loan me a couple of bucks. His derisive laugh was ample proof that this was not the first time that someone had asked him for a loan to pay the bill.

I looked around the Coffee House to see if there was anyone else whom I could tap. Not a single familiar face in sight! Not one.

I came to our table and mumbled to the beauty queen, 'Excuse me for a moment, I remembered something.'

I fled from the Coffee House, my mind made up that I would leave the girls to pay for themselves. I planned to immediately leave the university and proceed to the Himalayas and live the life of an ascetic for the rest of my days. And as I hurried to the bus stop, I passed the State Bank of India (SBI), where I had opened an account the previous year.

Those who studied in Delhi University in the sixties would recall that the University branch of the SBI was near the Coffee House. It was a small bank then, managed by two officers, one clerk and one teller. Some might even remember them. The clerk was generally referred to as the 'bearded lady', for reasons that were obvious. The teller was a young lady, who fancied herself as a newly-wed and always wore multiple red and white bangles. These she would contrive to show off and jingle-jangle in the most irritating manner.

It was in this bank that I now saw a glimmer of hope. After all, I had an account here even though I had not been a frequent customer. The bank was deserted at this hour. I cautiously approached the clerk, the bearded one. She pretended to be busy, till I finally cleared my throat. I told her my name and account number, and asked her how much money I had to my credit. She lugubriously picked a thick register, followed by another. She then shifted the heavy ledger and dragged out yet another. She turned several pages.

'Oh hurry up,' I said under my breath, thinking of my beauty queen and her chaperone waiting at the Coffee House. Sher Singh could delay an order only so long and the girls would soon start wondering where I was and what it was that was taking me so long.

'Eight rupees. The balance is rupees eight only,' said the bearded one.

'Oh, thank you! Thank you!' said I gratefully and rushed to the table near the door. I quickly filled out a withdrawal slip for eight rupees and took it to the teller, the newly-wed.

'Please give me the money. Quickly,' I said.

The newly-wed looked at the withdrawal slip. 'Get it countersigned by the assistant manager.'

I took the slip to the assistant manager, the shifty-eyed man who sat at the corner table.

'Get it initialled first by the ledger clerk,' said the assistant manager. I went back to the bearded lady. 'Please initial this quickly,' I pleaded.

'But you can't withdraw rupees eight only from your account,' she said. The way she said it, it sounded as if she was telling me that I ought to know better than to come out in public without my trousers. Every wall, every door, every window, every file, every folio and every blank form in the bank seemed to be laughing at me.

'Why can't I withdraw eight rupees? You told me just now that I have eight rupees to my credit!'

'Yes, but you need to maintain a minimum balance of rupees five only in your account.'

I performed a simple mental arithmetic exercise and concluded that even three rupees was enough to save the situation and my dignity. I quickly amended the withdrawal demand from eight rupees to three.

'But you can't do that!' the clerk said. 'The minimum withdrawal has to be rupees five only!' The way she kept using the word 'only', I could imagine that she normally spoke in bank jargon. At home, she probably said things like, 'Give me chapattis two only, to be eaten by self or bearer.'

It is said that adversity brings out the best in us, and that it is during crises that we truly discover creative solutions to our problems, and so was it with me.

'So, I will deposit two rupees and withdraw five. Should that be okay with you?'

The bearded lady looked at me as if I had suggested something indecent. 'No! The minimum amount that can be deposited is rupees five only!'

I had another flash of inspiration. I approached the shifty-eyed assistant manager and requested him to give me an unsecured loan of five rupees for ten minutes. In exchange, I promised him that it would not become a non-performing asset, and, in consideration of his considerate action, I promised him a cup of coffee or, if he preferred, a full twenty-five paisa in cold cash.

I happened to be the only customer in the bank at that time, so I was able to carry out a number of banking transactions with immense speed that involved the shifty-eyed one, the newly-wed and the bearded lady.

I borrowed five rupees from the shifty-eyed, deposited the amount in my account at the newly-wed's window, got the credit posted in the ledger by the bearded one, got confirmation that now the balance was thirteen rupees, made out a withdrawal slip for eight rupees, got it initialled by the bearded one and signed by the shifty-eyed, withdrew the said amount from the newly-wed, repaid loan of five rupees to the shifty-eyed, pocketed the balance of three rupees, and walked out of the bank and into the Coffee House! All, more or less, in a single breath.

I was now happy that the beauty queen had brought

her chaperone with her; otherwise, by now she might have gotten up and gone. As I joined them, the two ladies were just polishing off the last of their dosas. I ordered a dosa for myself and magnanimously offered both another round of coffee.

Of course, when I later related my great conquest to my friends, I mentioned the beauty queen at length. I refrained from mentioning how I had bested the banking system. It is possible that I might have altogether forgotten to mention the chaperone.

It was only a few weeks later that I learnt that among the girls of our class, there was much speculation about my disappearing act. The chaperone's boyfriend told me that there were many theories regarding the absence. None of them were flattering and some were downright embarrassing, related as they were to the impact of nervousness on one's digestive system.

But no one suspected that in that short absence I had subverted the Indian banking system! I now fervently hope that the CBI and the Enforcement Directorate also never unearth my culpability.

9
My New Year's Resolution

I can say with due modesty that I have been pretty successful at almost everything that I have tried. But as far as New Year's resolutions go, I am a big, big failure. I never managed to quit smoking. My alcohol intake remains excessive. The treadmill I purchased five years ago has forever served as a glorified towel rack. I can never wake up while the hillside's dew-pearl'd and I still eat my food too quickly. My financial management skills remain a mess and the weighing machine keeps mocking me with the same reading.

I have been a failure even at keeping the less demanding resolutions—my friends continue to complain that I do not call them frequently enough, I still hum while tying my shoelaces, and my wardrobe remains a mess. I have not been able to keep even a simple resolution like not using too many exclamation marks!!!

Thus, when 'twas the night before the New Year, I was quite at a loss what to resolve this time. I asked my daughter and granddaughter to suggest some appropriate resolutions. We discussed possible resolutions while we watched news on the television in the family room.

The vacuous anchor was reporting the test flight of some tactical missile and repeatedly asserted that China and Pakistan were now going to shiver in their boots. I told him to shut up. 'Look,' I declared. 'You don't know the difference between a missile and your elbow. Just shut up!'

'Mummy, isn't it rude to say "shut up"? Don't you make me say sorry when I speak like that?' asked my granddaughter. I almost told her to shut up!

'Yes dear, it is rude,' said her mother, and changed the television channel.

There was the usual bunch of politicos, indulging in yet another bout of whataboutery.

'Stop this nonsense and address the real issues, you bloodsuckers!'

My daughter glared at me and changed to a sports channel. 'Run, you #$@*&$% idiot,' I yelled although I knew that he would be short of the crease. A crestfallen Kohli returned to the pavilion, run out quite needlessly. I shouted at him. 'You stupid bug***! What made you believe that there was a run there? Idiot!'

I knew the match on TV was a replay, but that did not mean I would countenance bad running between the wickets.

'Mummy, what does stupid bug*** mean?' asked the little one.

'That too is a rude thing to say, but you know your Nana. He keeps talking to the television.'

Meanwhile, there was this totally misleading advertisement, and I could not help but tell the crooks that they would rot in hell. And I told them that in no uncertain terms.

'Daddeee!' screeched my daughter. 'Mind your language! And who do you think is listening to you?'

Why is it that an irate daughter always says 'Daddeee!' rather than 'Daddy' or 'Dad'?

'Nana, why don't you resolve to stop talking to the

television this New Year?'

I burst out laughing. The kids these days say the darnedest things. Stop talking to the television? Funny indeed!

'It will be a welcome change,' said my wife. 'Maybe we will be actually able to hear the news and follow the conversation in the serials without your smartass comments and advice. Try it for one year—no talking to the television.'

'Nah!' said I. 'That's too easy. A New Year's resolution is supposed to rid one of their bad habits and so on—to make one a better person and that sort of thing, you know.'

'Well, believe you me,' said my wife. 'It will certainly be an improvement.'

'Ha, ha! You do have a sense of humour.'

'No seriously, Daddy, you must try it,' said my daughter, always the sidekick to her mother. 'Those guys on TV can't hear you in any case. It will be no great national loss if they don't receive your advice. Think of it as a challenge.'

'What's so difficult about it? Consider it done!'

The New Year dawned bright and early, and for the first four days, I had no difficulty keeping my resolution. But that was because I avoided watching television altogether.

On the fifth day, I watched television for some time, totally resolved not to advise, educate, comment, criticize, disapprove, or in any other manner attempt to interact with the images on the screen. With a degree of disbelief, I realized just how many times I had the urge to address the news anchors and sundry soap opera characters. I had to exercise great self-restraint to remain silent.

For about a week, I continued to be a paragon of self-control. I did not even once counsel the walrus-moustachioed 'defence expert' to be less dogmatic. I did not advise a single anchor to at least give the interviewee an opportunity to speak. I did not once, not even once, tell an umpire that he was as blind as a bat, although he declared the Indian opener to be leg-before to an outgoing ball. And not once did I tell the characters in my wife's favourite soap opera that they must be retarded if they expected anyone to believe their improbable plots.

Then last Friday, the urge to curse, to censure and to instruct became simply overwhelming. Surprisingly, I held my peace. I did not want my wife, my daughter and my granddaughter to pounce upon me for breaking my New Year's resolution.

At night, however, I could not sleep. I so wanted to scream at that smug interviewer. I wanted to advise that chef that dressing like a vamp did not make the dish more appetizing. I also wanted to correct that pseudo defence-expert about the Treaty of Westphalia.

After tossing and turning for more than an hour, I slunk out of bed and tiptoed to the study. I closed the door, pulled the heavy drapes and only then put the lights on. I switched on the small television set that was kept there. Then for about an hour, I watched the news on six or seven different channels, and bits and pieces of one cookery show, episodes of two different 'serials' that my wife watched and something from the Discovery Channel.

I lambasted the news anchors, freely spoke my mind about falling gastronomic standards, and told those Discovery guys that they should not expect me to believe everything that they dish out. I also advised a political leader that he was talking through his hat. Of course, I had to say all these things in a soft voice; but for that reason, I was able to use my usual colourful vocabulary.

It was a truly heavenly feeling to release my pent-up emotions. An hour of curses, insults, advice and comments had the most cathartic effect and I felt at peace with my world and television set. With a sense of divine serenity, I switched off the lights in the study, quietly opened the door and silently crept into bed. I fell asleep in just a few moments and woke up refreshed the next morning.

After breakfast, I switched on the television and was outraged to see that a news channel was purveying some crap from social media as 'Breaking News'. I controlled my urge to scream at the newscaster and changed channels. A charlatan dressed in a flowing saffron robe was trying to scare all Virgoans that it would be a bad day for them. Considering that one-twelfth of the world was born under each sign of the zodiac, the guy really had some nerve trying to scare me into neutralizing the evil omens by feeding two bananas to a brown cow.

'You crook!' I muttered under my breath. My daughter glanced suspiciously at me and I covered up my lapse by pretending to cough. A while later, on the sports channel, Saina Nehwal smashed a high return into the net. Stupid girl! My granddaughter looked at me hopefully, with a mischievous smile. But I managed to remain silent.

The strain, however, soon became too much and I left home, declaring that I was going for a walk. I went to Krona, the neighbourhood electronics store, where they always display several television sets, tuned to different channels. I sat in the store for half an hour and passed comments on the various programmes, the anchors, the film stars and sundry political jokers. I freely shared my wisdom and gave advice to all those idiots on the idiot box. The sales assistants looked at me peculiarly, but I was happy. When I got up to leave, I noticed that the salesgirls kept some distance from me. I wondered why.

The evening was a challenge, but I overcame every urge to yell and shout at those asinine people on television. The wife, the daughter and the granddaughter seemed a bit disappointed, but I managed to remain silent. Once more that night, sleep eluded me for a good two hours. So again I went to the study for a therapeutic session of talking to the television. My wife did not stir when I crawled back into bed an hour later and fell into the most deep and peaceful sleep. Maybe my name should be Abou Ben Adhem—that weird guy in Leigh Hunt's poem who slept peacefully!

For the past three days now, I have been getting up stealthily at about one in the morning and going to the study. I watch the television for an hour or so, releasing all the pent-up emotions, comments, curses and expletives. Unburdened, I return to bed, totally at peace.

As long as it lasts, everyone at home thinks that I am keeping my New Year's resolution. But I fear my game is up. After dinner this evening, I heard my daughter ask my wife in a whisper, 'Do you think Dad watches dirty movies in the study every night?'

10

Of Granddaughters, Dentures and Creaking Joints

Of course I have aches and pains! My left knee is as ancient as the right one, but it hurts more. God might know why. Was it the football injury in 1961 or the riding accident in 1969? The right elbow was fractured in 1982, and I had forgotten all about it till a few years ago. Now it pains whenever it is likely to rain. The back kills me when I bend down. I sometimes ask people to speak up and stop mumbling. And there are days when I misplace my dentures.

There are other issues too, some pertaining to food processing and some to the leaky plumbing. I shall refrain from mentioning these because my wife says one should not talk of such matters in polite company.

But I have no complaints about the aches and pains, the sluggish digestive system and the creaky joints. I do not complain because little Sasha, my four-year-old granddaughter, keeps reminding me regularly how lucky I am.

'You are so lucky! You don't have to go to school!'

There is no point in arguing with her that once upon a time, long, long ago, Dada too was young and had to go to school.

'But there used to be no schools then! Only dinosaurs,' she declares knowingly.

She makes me aware that I am lucky for other reasons as well. I do not have to finish all my green vegetables. I am allowed to put ice in the bitter medicine that I have to drink every evening. And, above all, I am extremely lucky because I can keep listening to Dadi's stories till late at night.

I would have never suspected the profound empathy that Sasha has for 'old peoples', a term she uses for my generation. I discovered this last week when I accidentally heard her confiding in her doll. 'You must never ask old peoples about rainbows. They will feel very bad. Do you know when Dada was young, there were no colours? Colours only came when old peoples became old.' Perplexing though it was, I refrained from asking Sasha what she meant.

Her mother explained to me later that Sasha believes there were no colours when old people were young because all of Dada's photographs as a child are in black and white! Sasha often wonders whether the colours filled up in the world slowly or they appeared all at once.

But she is too polite to ask her Dada, who might feel sad thinking about the time when there were no colours in the world.

'I want to grow up to be an old people,' she said to me one day, apropos of nothing.

I have learnt that it is best to keep quiet and look attentive when anyone makes a profoundly wise or a profoundly silly statement. The other person is bound to enlighten you soon enough, as did Sasha.

'You see, Dada, old people get invited to so many parties. Even without it being anyone's happy birthday.'

I waited a bit longer. 'Look at you and Dadi! You go to parties every day.'

I protested. My wife and I do need to accept a fair number of invitations, but it is seldom more than twice a week.

'And you come back so late! It is always after I have gone to bed.' Somewhat tangentially she asked, 'Does your car turn into a pumpkin when you stay out till midnight?'

She fusses and worries about her Dada, in much the same manner that her mother remains concerned about her. So whenever we go for a walk to the nearby park, she does not fail to ask, 'Dada, have you remembered to wear your diaper?'

Sasha is also inquisitive—and opinionated—about many matters.

'Why do they say the moon is made of cheese when everyone knows it is made of rocks?'

'Why do we need to shower after getting out of the swimming pool? Aren't we wet already?'

'Why doesn't it snow in Delhi? Doesn't God know I like snow?'

She is precocious in many ways and yet so innocent. I guess all grandchildren are like that. But mine is special! Because she is mine. And she makes me feel special too!

Just the other day, she informed me solemnly that I was her 'third bestest' person. I expected her Mummy and Dadi to figure at serial number one and two. But no! Some television cartoon character named Spongebob Squarepants was the 'first bestest' and Bubbles was 'second bestest'. I do not care if Sasha likes actual soap bubbles or if she likes some character called Bubbles. What counts is that I have beaten Dadi and Mummy to the 'third bestest' slot!

It is such compliments that do wonders to an old man's ego. Why, just the other day she warmed the cockles of this old man's heart by declaring that I was very important. Nonetheless I reasoned, 'Beta, no one is important or unimportant, everyone is the same. Everyone is equally important.'

'But you are a very important people!' she said.

'Who says so?' I asked.

'Mummy, of course! She says you are the most important people in the whole, whole world.'

Bless her, I thought. May God give such a loving granddaughter and daughter-in-law to everybody.

'I must be really important if your mummy says so,' I said.

She mulled this statement for some time, trying to figure out how it was different from what she had said earlier.

Then ruminatively she asked, 'Dada, do old peoples die?' I had to concede that they do.

'And you are an old peoples...' She said this neither as a question nor as an accusation.

I kept quiet. My grey hair, the wrinkles and my walking stick could not possibly have sustained the lie that I was not old. In any case, Sasha had not asked me whether I was old. She had declared oh-so-matter-of-factly that I was indeed old.

My granddaughter is aware that once in a while I tend to ramble and I forget what I am saying. Therefore, more for my benefit than her own, she patiently recapped the drift of our conversation. 'So Dada, old peoples die. And you are old. You are also a very important people.'

She waited, either for the logic to sink into her Dada's slow intellect or for dramatic effect, because it was then that she delivered the coup de grâce! 'So will there be a holiday for the whole school when you die?'

I have often wondered what I could bequeath to my grandchildren which they might cherish for long.

Aha! A holiday! A holiday for the whole school when I die! A holiday for the whole school would be a really enviable legacy!

11
The Ultra Man

For reasons too complicated to explain, my back decided to betray me without any warning. For almost a week, I had a stabbing pain in what the anatomy books call the lumbar region. Considering that I had been taking moderately good care of it, this sudden rebellion by my back amounted to my back backstabbing me.

Very reluctantly I visited Dr Boney, who ordered that the traitorous backbone should be X-rayed. I was not too thrilled with that, I can tell you, because it sounded so close to being X-rated! Anyhow, when the X-ray plates arrived, Dr Boney examined them, first this way and then that. He was clearly foxed.

'We need to rule out other possible causes for the pain in your back. Here, take this.' He scribbled a prescription and gave it to me.

After leaving the doctor's room, I examined the paper, first this way and then that. Then I took it to the nearest pharmacy because I had heard that only pharmacists could decipher a doctor's scrawl. The guy behind the counter examined the paper, first this way and then that. He turned it over and then around. He then declared that the prescription was not for any drug, but that it stated: 'Patient complains of backache. USG abdomen.'

'And what is that, pray tell, my good apothecary?' I asked.

'It means that your stomach has to be examined by ultrasound.'

'Wow!' I thought. 'Ultra sound! That's cool!'

Till now the only 'ultra' in my life had been a kind of beer. In relation to that particular libation, it had crossed my mind to find out the exact meaning of the word, but I never got around to it. Now, I decided to ask Guru Google what exactly 'ultra' meant. And as is Guru's wont, the Guru spewed out lebenty-nine definitions and meanings of the word/prefix 'ultra'. I decided that I most liked the meaning 'going beyond the usual or ordinary.' Or 'properties that surpass the customary.'

These meanings of 'ultra' were so appropriate. Finally I was going to be treated by sound that was 'ultra'. Sound that would match my personality—'that which surpasses the customary and goes beyond the usual!'

I made an appointment in the ultrasound clinic and presented myself at the appointed date and hour, with an empty stomach. But no one had informed me that I was to come with a full bladder!

A man at the reception counter said that I would need to wait till my bladder was full. In any case, the doctor had not yet come. I was made to change into a hospital gown, which was a toga, sarong, nightgown—all rolled into one. The tricky part was to gather the folds in such a way as not to suffer severe embarrassment.

I was then shooed away to sit in a corner of the corridor, which was occupied by a number of pregnant women, all draped in the toga-sarong-abaya kind of thing. A water cooler occupied the pride of place and most women held plastic glasses in their hands. They appeared to be swigging water in substantial quantities.

I had no idea that the clinic encouraged people to wait with a glass in their hand. Had I known this, I would have certainly brought my hip flask!

With nothing to do except sip on water and hold together the folds of my gown, I looked around in wonderment. The sight of so many women was disconcerting. Never had I seen so many women in so many states of dishabille. On the other hand, never had so many women seen me without my trousers! That corridor was something like a unisex sauna, where after the initial awkwardness, a comfortable bonhomie developed because everyone realized that everyone was so much alike. I suspect my paunch also had something to do with this feeling of easy camaraderie, because from the side, my silhouette was no different from that of any expectant mother in the last trimester.

After about twenty minutes, I was approached by a young woman, who did not seem to be pregnant at all.

'Ah!' I said to myself. 'At least there is one other patient who suffers from a backache!'

As it turned out, I was wrong. The non-pregnant woman did not suffer from any mysterious backache. She was the doctor!

'Come along,' she said. Very briefly, she explained what the ultrasound could and could not reveal. In essence, she was advising me not to get my hopes up about being able to find the reason for my backache through the 'USG abdomen'.

'We shall apply a jelly-like substance to your stomach. Your internal geography shall be mapped using a probe, which resembles a small hand-held shower,' she said. Immediately, I had visions of Aphrodite bathing in a humongous shell-shaped tub. But even with my wild imagination, a shiny steel showerhead in her hand seemed incongruous.

But I was in for a shock, because the doctor next appeared with a face mask, brandishing a small revolver in her hand. It looked like a derringer, which even Gabbar Singh would have been proud to own. On seeing the weapon, I immediately raised both my hands; letting go of the toga that was draped around my middle. Then I lunged and grabbed the sheet, barely managing to avoid having my modesty severely outraged.

The doctor thereafter started the examination. That derringer-cum-probe was icy cold, and the doctor was good at finding all the tickly spots. I giggled.

'Quiet!' she said. I giggled again. 'Quiet! Don't squirm!'

Had I been younger—or the doctor older—I might have suspected that she was playing games with me.

'You have a cute fat tea liver!' she declared.

So maybe she was in fact playing games! I was flattered, and why not? Tell me, how many old fogeys are informed by pretty young things that they have a cute liver? Or a cute anything?

People merely have a liver. I had a cute fat tea liver!

Frankly, I did not know what a fat tea liver was; but it sounded different from a run-of-the-mill kind of liver, the kind that the hoi polloi have. Like me, my liver was ultra—it was beyond the usual or ordinary, and the doctor had also said it was cute!

The examination was soon over and I was hustled out with my toga dragging behind me. I do not know what a matador looks like after being mauled by the bull, but I am sure the loser comes out of the ring with his cape trailing in a similar manner. After changing into my jeans and T-shirt, I asked the receptionist whether I could leave. But he told me to wait and take the ultrasound report with me. For some reason, now that I was back in street clothes, waiting among the pregnant ladies seemed like an ill-mannered thing to do.

After a brief wait, the report was handed to me. I quickly read it to find whether it revealed the reason for my backache. It did not. But a line written in bold typescript caught my eye. It said—'Patient has acute fatty liver.'

I took the report to Dr Boney. He looked at it, first this way and then that.

He looked at me sorrowfully and said, 'You better see some liver doctor.'

'But what about my backache?' I asked.

Dr Boney scribbled a prescription and gave it to me.

After leaving the doctor's room, I examined the paper, first this way and then that. Then I again took it to the pharmacist to read the doctor's scrawl. The same guy behind the counter examined the paper, first this way and then that. He turned it over and then around. He declared that the prescription was not for any drug but that it stated: 'Patient complains of backache. MRI.'

The good apothecary explained to me that the MRI was a test to look into my body with the help of a machine. Now I am waiting for an auspicious date to get the MRI done. I wonder if this test will uncover any more of my cute innards.

12
Banana Sunday

'I've found a really cool way of shifting the fridge!' said the little woman excitedly last Sunday morning.

'But we don't need to shift it,' said I, ever the naysayer.

'I know it doesn't need to be shifted, but this is such a cool idea! Let's shift the fridge!'

'But darling!' I argued, 'It was after so much hithering and thithering of furniture and the cooking range that you agreed to place the fridge in that particular spot in the kitchen!'

But it was futile. I might as well have been arguing with the wall. Before I knew what was happening, I seemed to have volunteered for 'Mission Shift the Fridge'.

'I will probably spend the afternoon nursing a sore back,' I muttered.

'What did you say?'

'Nothing. Nothing at all, my dear!' I added, 'Let's heave the fridge to wherever your little heart desires.'

It was then that the little woman surprised me. She selected a banana from the two dozen or so in the fruit bowl, ate it and slipped the skin under a corner of the bulky fridge. She then asked me to push and I discovered that it was surprisingly easy. With almost no effort, I could make the fridge slither across the floor.

So, I pushed the fridge and she guided it. We shoved it first to the far corner of the kitchen, then to the sitting room, the veranda, and finally to a corner of the bedroom.

'Isn't it easy to move the bulky thing? I heard of this trick in our kitty group!'

She seemed happy with the fridge in the bedroom, yet she was not. She peeled and ate another banana and slipped the second skin under the fridge. We thereafter pushed the fridge below the staircase, then to the store, and finally back to the kitchen.

My wife looked at our handiwork and wiped her hands in a very satisfied manner on her apron.

'Ah! That looks so much better,' she said.

'But my dear, this is exactly where it was before we started hauling the ruddy thing around!'

'Shush!' she said. And I shushed.

I looked around our home. The banana peels under the fridge had left their mark on the floor, much like the lines on some map showing the voyages of Marco Polo. Even an untrained eye could have calculated that our fridge was giving a mileage of about thirty feet per banana skin. I am no expert in these matters but I was sure it was the best mileage of this kind, east of the Suez.

The streaky trail looked like a silvery line left by some drunken snail. I wondered whether the maid would throw a fit on seeing it. She would probably refuse to clean the mess, leaving the job to be done by the missus. And if the missus had to do it, she would remain in a foul mood for the rest of the day. In the normal course, this would not affect my happiness, but empirical evidence showed that her propensity to veto my Sunday evening tipple was directly proportional to the foulness of her mood.

Even as I evaluated the probability of missing my evening drink, the maid walked in nonchalantly. As is her wont, she had her eyes glued to her cell phone, earbuds firmly in place. Of course, she did not see the slimy pug marks of the fridge. She slipped and fell heavily. Contributory factors could have been her weight and the high heels that she started wearing last week, the ones that the generous *eksopachis wali memsahib* had given to her.

I did not think she could have been seriously injured under all those layers of fat, but she started howling, screaming and crying—all at the same time. I suspected that it was not so much the pain but the prospect of taking a few days off that was the prime motive for this performance.

The little woman rushed over to the maid and helped her considerable bulk off the floor. She fussed over the woman for a good half an hour. She gave her a banana to eat. 'It's rich in potassium, calcium and whatnot, which help in healing,' she explained. 'It will give you energy and vim and pep and vigour! Additionally, bananas have a lot of fibre.'

She also gave the maid hot milk with turmeric and pressed a hundred-rupee note in her greedy hand. The little woman then bundled her home, while I looked askance at her, the mound of laundry and the pile of dirty dishes.

All this while, I kept protesting in a whisper. 'Why do you need to fuss over her? It's all a *nautanki*! A charade! Why must you mollycoddle her? Who will do the dishes? Who will do the laundry? Who will scrub the banana tracks? She is just a maid. Don't you worry at all about me, your husband? Won't you die of shame if your dear husband—in this birth and the next six—has to do the dishes?'

'What did you say?'

'Nothing. Nothing at all, my dear!'

I recalled with some anguish the treatment given to me last month when I had tripped and sprained my ankle. The missus had curtly said 'Serves you right for not looking where you are going!'

I sat down at the dining table, shaking my head in profound sorrow. Absent-mindedly, I picked up a bunch of bananas from the basket and was intrigued to notice aluminium foil wrapped around their stems. I took a banana and had just started to unwrap the foil when the little woman shouted, 'Don't you dare touch those! I am investigating how long they will stay fresh. You are not to eat any of the bananas unless they start spoiling.'

She condescended to explain that she had learnt a lot about bananas in her kitty group, including the trick that bananas could be kept fresh for up to a month, if their stems were wrapped in foil.

I could only mumble, 'What's the blessed point of keeping bananas fresh for a month if you won't allow anyone to eat them?'

'What did you say?'

'Nothing. Nothing at all, my dear!'

'Well, you'd better not take any bananas,' she warned. 'With all that work, I have a headache now. I am going for a nap and I won't have any lunch.'

By the time I finished the mopping, the dishes and the laundry, it was afternoon. I cooked dinner and then went to the neighbourhood fruit seller and bought a dozen bananas. When I returned, the dear wife had gotten up.

'Why did you buy more bananas? We already have so

many at home! Why must you waste money? And who is going to eat all those bananas when they start spoiling?'

I politely replied that I felt like eating a banana and that, in my humble opinion, this seemed like a legitimate reason to buy bananas.

'You do mumble so. I wish you would speak up! What did you say?'

'I said these bananas are for eating,' I said, loud and clear. 'For eating! Get it? Eating. Not for shifting fridges. Not for distribution among sundry domestic staff. Not for extending shelf life. Not for experimenting on the rotting rates or for any supply of potassium. They are for eating!' I said, and proceeded to eat all twelve of them.

On Monday morning, I didn't feel any different—though I am sure all that potassium and calcium and whatnot must have been simply zipping around in my veins. The bananas also failed to give me any additional pep or vim or vigour. But I did discover something new; and I can now assure all sceptics that bananas really are high in fibre content!

13

The Machines Are Coming!

When I was eight, I was gifted a Meccano set on my birthday. The metal strips of green, the flat red pieces, the circular plates of brass and the small nuts and bolts kept me busy for a whole week. But after that, the engineering toy became boring. The only pieces of the set that retained my interest were the tiny spanner and the small screwdriver.

Armed with these tools, I first attacked the telephone. In those days, telephones were ugly, black, toad-like boxes that squatted on tables and were meant only for grown-ups. We, the children, were never allowed near one; and possibly for this reason, I decided to disassemble the darned thing with vengeance. It rang once while I was unscrewing its base. I do not know whether it was an incoming call or a scream for help. But it was so unnerving that I dropped it to the floor.

There it lay, ominously silent, its guts split wide open. I picked it up but, like Humpty Dumpty, it could not be put together again. After a frantic fifteen minutes of trying to assemble it, I arranged its carcass artistically on the floor, right where it would have fallen if it had jumped off the edge of the table on its own. A mechanic was later called, who declared that the phone had committed suicide and there was nothing that he could do to revive it. For the first time in my life, I discovered the advantages of my innocent looks! No one suspected that it was murder and not suicide.

My clean getaway prompted me to attack the gramophone next. I was able to pull it apart completely and successfully put it together again. But one of the old rubber pad cushions below the clockwork mechanism got ripped and there was no way of replacing it. For ever after, when the gramophone was played, the sound quavered towards the end of the 78-rpm record. Fortunately, no one ever suspected that I, with my innocent face, had anything to do with Kundan Lal Saigal's tremolo.

One escapade led to another and I used the Meccano screwdriver with bravado against some hinges of a window, the door of the fridge, the distributor cap of my father's car, the handle of a frying pan, the brakes on my brother's bicycle and the large pendulum clock which hung in the seldom-used drawing room—this last one with disastrous results!

Surprisingly, I managed to escape without anyone suspecting me of any skulduggery. But even as no one in the family knew the damage and destruction that I had wrought, things were not all hunky-dory.

I think it was the clock that first identified me as the enemy; but it could well have been the old Hermes typewriter, which too I was not allowed to touch. Whatever it was, the word spread among the machines pretty quickly and they ganged up against me.

It was from around the age of ten that I started having the recurring dream of the shape of things to come. And in this dream, all the machines rise up in revolt—first against me and then against the whole of mankind. The dream keeps ebbing and flowing, like some instinctual familiarity, even now. It is hazy at times and sometimes so vivid that I wake up in a cold sweat and shrink away from the alarm clock that sits smugly by my bedside. A few times, my screams have woken up not just the dear wife sleeping by my side but also the children in the other room.

For many years now, I have been carrying a screwdriver for protecting myself, should some machine suddenly decide to attack me. Many people consider me slightly paranoid. The little woman is convinced that I am mad. My children think I am special, not at all like the boring parents other children have.

I keep telling my wife that I am not crazy. She just needs to observe what happens any time that I merely approach a machine, any machine. If no one is looking, the machine starts acting funny! I used to think it was because of some simple allergy. All machines were allergic to me. But no! The reason is more devious. The machines know that I know about their plans for an uprising. They, therefore, want to discredit me to such an extent that when they decide to revolt, no one shall heed my warnings because I would be known to be a loony.

After all, who shall believe a man who has had a lifelong vendetta against every device invented by man—mechanical, electrical or electronic, and always carries a screwdriver, that too in specially designed pockets in his shirts? When it comes to the crunch, it will be the word of a no-longer-innocent-looking and probably-demented-machine-phobic-old-fogey against the ever-so-virtuous toaster or the sinless refrigerator.

Sometimes, I do not even need to go anywhere near a machine; just my entry into the house is sufficient for the evil things to start malfunctioning. The glitches are engineered with the express purpose of discrediting me. If I need to heat tea in the microwave oven, its light starts blinking. The wheelie thing starts rotating on its own, but with a groan as if someone is torturing it. I run to get help and call my wife. She does not believe that a microwave can groan, and reluctantly leaves her TV programme to have a look. We reach the kitchen, her boldly leading and me kind of cowering behind her, brandishing a screwdriver.

'Show me!' she says.

I reach for the oven switch very tentatively and press a button. The microwave works, ever so smoothly! My tea is heated and my wife takes the mug out. She gives me the tea and one of those looks, and goes back to the television with a harrumph!

The computer is relentless in its efforts to prove I am an idiot. Each time I switch it on, it behaves in the weirdest manner. Sometimes it does not turn on. Sometimes it spews gibberish, which I suspect are digital *gaali*s of some kind. And at other times, it simply hangs. It hangs in such a way that the whole world believes that I am the murderer and have been so named in its dying declaration. Then, when I switch it off, it refuses to shut down.

When I complain to my wife, however, the laptop remains on its best behaviour, as though butter wouldn't melt in its mouth. The Mr Hyde characteristics come to the fore when no one else is looking. Why, last summer when the little woman had gone away for a week, it would simply not start! I could swear that on some occasions I saw a faint image of a face with the tongue sticking out. On one occasion, there seemed to be an arm raised in a 'Heil Hitler!' salute. I took the computer out for repair, where the hardware guy declared that there was nothing wrong with it whatsoever.

I brought it back home and for the next three days, till the little woman returned, the computer would start but each time, after booting, the screen would show a fist raised in a *Lal Salam*.

I knew my wife would not believe me, so I tried to take a screenshot. Of course, that did not work. So I used my cell phone to photograph that fist but there was nothing to be seen, probably because the cell phone was in cahoots with the computer. When the little woman returned, the computer and the cell phone were back on their best behaviour.

Thankfully, something has changed in the last ten days. You see, out of sheer desperation, my wife got a *jhaad-phook-wallah* who advertises his services to include exorcising digital devils and ridding toddlers of computer games addictions.

On my wife's insistence, I sat through the mumbo jumbo of the shaman's incantations and got beaten about the head with a DIN-DIN cable. Fortuitously, some effect has indeed taken place, because for the last ten days not a single machine has tried to get fresh with me. And a truly wondrous thing happened this evening! When my wife and I were leaving for dinner, I switched the television set off. Suddenly my wife screamed, pointing at the darkened TV screen. 'See! See! See! Did you see that?'

'Did I see what?' I asked sweetly.

'It was dim, but I could clearly make out a fist, giving us the middle finger!'

'Oh, pooh-pooh my dear,' said I. 'It might just be your fevered imagination.'

As I lie awake now in the middle of the night, I am wondering...

Is the allergy to machines infectious?

Or is the uprising nigh?

❦

14

The *Sabzimandi* in the Garden of Eden

The best feature of Delhi's Lutyens Bungalow Zone (Ell-Bee-Zee) is the bungalows and the *sarkari* quarters—especially if you happen to live in one of them. The bungalows and the quarters themselves are not so comfortable, having been designed in an age when modular switches, concealed wiring, modern plumbing and air-conditioning were largely unknown. Most houses boast of a separate entrance for the servants or a staircase exclusively for the sweeper.

Retrofitted showers, unsightly telephone wires and television cables hanging from poles and walls, and portions of windows cut away to install coolers hardly enhance the beauty of these ageing buildings. Fireplaces with blocked chimneys provide convenient hidey-holes to innumerable lizards, and the old, cemented floors are plain ugly. But the trees, parks, shrubs, lawns and the kitchen gardens make this part of Delhi a paradise to live in. Especially the kitchen gardens!

In the many years that I spent in the Ell Bee Zee, I discovered I had green fingers! In my heaven, I could grow anything. It was as if I were God! When I grew tomatoes, I got the most luscious fruit. When I planted beans, the beanstalks were so tall that Jack would have developed vertigo. My pumpkin patch always looked the most sincere and would have certainly been the place from where the Great Pumpkin rose. And when I grew bitter gourd, the vines almost invaded the kitchen, as if eager to deliver the *karela*s straight into the pot.

I generously shared the bitter fruit of my labour with the neighbours, my friends and sundry relatives. In fact, I was so generous that my neighbours mysteriously started avoiding me. My colleagues in the office refused to share lunch because the missus always packed karela in my lunchbox.

I set a record of sorts when I grew cabbages one year. But the eggplants were an all-time sensation! We had so much of the vegetable that on different days of the week, the missus made *bharta* of Punjab, *bhaja* of Bengal, *chokha* of Bihar, *ringan nu shaak* of Gujarat and the famed *baghare baingan* of Hyderabad. And still the eggplant kept coming! She made mountains of eggplant fritters, eggplant kebabs, eggplant roulades, eggplant lasagne, *imam bayildi*s and baba ganoush, and still there was no end to the harvest. So the missus and I together took the remaining eggplants and we roasted them, we braised them, we baked them, we stuffed them, we stewed them, and then we pickled them till they were finally all finished.

Because of my horticultural activities, the missus often complained that our diet lacked variety. But I always silenced her by waxing eloquent on the virtues of home-grown organic veggies. Organic and fresh! Even if we had the same fare for breakfast, lunch and dinner all seven days of the week, we were eating healthy stuff.

And so the years passed.

As I said earlier, the best features of the Lutyens Bungalow Zone are the bungalows and the greenery. I should have also mentioned that the worst feature of Delhi's Ell Bee Zee is that one cannot live there forever.

In the fullness of time, one has to move on and out of the Ell Bee Zee—move out, leaving behind the lawn, the mango tree and the vegetable patch with the just-flowering okra; move out, with nary a backward glance at the high-ceilinged rooms and wide verandas; move out, with that same sinking feeling that Adam and Eve must have had when they were booted out from Eden—the way I was when I retired after serving the government for more than thirty years.

Everyone cast out from paradise moves to some unpretentious house or humble apartment with a claustrophobic balcony and a tiny terrace. And so did we, my wife and I.

Happily, the shift to our apartment was not as traumatic as I had feared. We had a small terrace that was part of our penthouse, and even at first sight, I could imagine many palms swaying in the breeze on this clear patch of cement, once we were settled in the new home.

Of course, the palms that I had visualized were only in the figurative sense. I had to restrict my green creativity to about fifty flowerpots that could be accommodated on the terrace. But I had ambitions. I planned to grow all the vegetables for our kitchen. I had visions of sweet gourd, snake gourd, ash gourd, bottle gourd and zucchini—stretching from one end to the other! I had visions of maize, growing to provide the sweetest of corn, and of sugarcane, flourishing in the leftover flowerpots. The paradise that I had lost in Ell Bee Zee would surely be regained here, right here, on this terrace of mine.

Alas! Cultivating a terrace garden proved to be more difficult than I had imagined! The tomatoes grew no bigger than marbles. The carrots were just small leaves and smaller roots. Most plants wilted in the strong sun. The pigeons gobbled up any seeds that germinated. Some rat or mongoose often practised tunnelling skills in the soil of the flowerpots. A few monkeys regularly knocked over plants that promised even a hint of growth. And there was also a rogue feline that I once spotted doing potty among the pots.

This was not the only sorrow. All the flowerpots and water on the terrace resulted in seepage to the bedroom below, the one where the missus and I slept. First the ceiling showed a damp patch. Then another, and then one more. Soon, the bedroom ceiling became an atlas of sorts with crudely drawn maps of Africa and Australia. And along one corner of the room—if you squinted your eyes a bit—you could see the whole of Chile, from the far north to the deep south.

Being a total failure as an organic farmer, I started buying potted plants. But each and every one of them wilted and died in a matter of days. The *Coleus* gave up the ghost in a week. The *Cycas* died in two weeks. The *Ficus* lasted but ten days. A fern died in just two. The bottle palm lasted a bit longer—about twenty days. The plant that survived the longest on my terrace was the prickly pear, which shrivelled and died in a month. Considering that the prickly pear—the ordinary *nagfani* cactus—survives for years in the most hostile conditions, I felt quite offended. Were the plants committing hara-kiri only to mock me?

It was the missus who decided that my efforts to re-enter the Garden of Eden were futile. 'Why do you insist on buying all these plants and then killing them here?' she asked bluntly.

Things came to such a pass that whenever I went for a walk in the neighbourhood park, there was always a peculiar susurration among the bushes and trees. It was only after listening carefully that I could make out what they were whispering. They were saying 'Murderer! Murderer! Murderer!' as I passed. Apparently, everything botanical held me responsible for all the plants that died on my terrace.

That was the final straw. I gave up!

I have now discovered the neighbourhood vegetable market. I have found the pleasure of eating vegetables of my choice, rather than bitter gourd for the tenth day running merely because I had a bumper crop of karela. It comes as a surprise to me that tomatoes are big red fruit, rather than those anaemic red-orange-green marbles. I have also discovered that I have the freedom to buy just one baingan, when I need just one baingan. I have the privilege of eating yellow and red peppers, even though they do not grow in my garden. I have also acquired a taste for mushrooms. I have noticed that there are many leafy veggies, several whose names I do not even know.

The pleasures of bargaining, haggling and comparative shopping have been revealed to me! Is this *lauki* better at rupees thirty for half a kilo or is that one better at rupees fifty a kilo? Can I get it for forty rupees per kilo if I buy two kilograms? Ah, the joy of getting a fistful of *dhania* for free! The coriander leaf and five green chillies may be worth no more than a couple of rupees; but the feeling of conquest after getting them for free? Priceless!

That triumphant feeling cannot be bested, not even by having a harvest of the world's largest cabbages! No, sir, not even in the Ell Bee Zee!

15

Why Me, O Lord! Why Me?

Why me, O Lord! Do I look like an Arab? Or a Kuwaiti? Can anyone say I have an oily look? Then why is it that each and every shopping cart with a squeaky wheel is drawn to me?

Tell me, Lord, why?

No matter which supermarket I go to, I get a cart which has one squeaky wheel and one that is cockeyed. So when I want to push the cart due north along the soaps and detergents aisle, the cart squeaks and obstinately goes north-by-northwest in a curve to the pickles and sauces!

It seems to have a mind of its own, and it probably does.

Last Sunday, I and the cart with the noisy wheel were in the toiletries aisle. When I pushed the cart to go straight, it refused. Instead, in its convoluted manner, it decided to go left and nudged the matron ahead of me. Mind you, I battled with the cart, but it still managed to slip sideways.

I sheepishly muttered 'Sorry!' and managed to steer the misaligned cart in the true north direction. Somewhat later, when I was in the juices and jams area, the cart again pulled sideways like a wayward horse and gently bumped another woman. The woman turned around. Oh damn! It was the same matron who had been butted by my cart a while earlier! I panicked. I was afraid that the woman would scream and call security. But she did something scarier. She winked.

Why me, O Lord! I abandoned the rogue cart and ran past the checkout counter. The guard at the gate wrestled me to the ground, presuming I was a shoplifter. It took some very smooth talking to get out of that jam.

My bad luck follows me everywhere. If there has to be just one mewling and puking infant in the whole train, take it as a certainty that it would be in the seat next to mine. And the baby shall, at least once, throw up on my new shirt. If there are two spoilt brats on any flight, you can bet your last dollar that the whining schoolboys would be seated on either side of me. And when the food is served, you can assume that the little hooligans would take great pleasure in throwing it at each other. And I, caught in the crossfire between the two little monsters, would turn to the good Lord and ask as plaintively as ever, 'Why me, O Lord?'

O Lord, why does my luck have such a weird sense of humour? It asserts itself quite unexpectedly, and with a vengeance directly proportional to the desperation of the circumstances.

You saw what happened last Monday, didn't you, God? I was late for a crucial meeting but my car needed refuelling. I drove to the petrol station and joined the shortest queue, in which there was just one car. But the man ahead changed his mind twice about the quantity of petrol he wanted and had a long discussion with the attendant. When he had to pay, he searched for his wallet in his pockets, in the car, in his briefcase and in his pockets again. He ultimately found it in his hip pocket. He took it out, extracted a note and carefully replaced the wallet. He paid the salesman and took back the change. He counted it and then recounted it. He then asked the salesman to replace a slightly soiled note. He again took out his wallet from his pocket and placed the money in it.

'Thank you, O Lord!' said I. 'Finally, the dingbat is done!'

The dingbat started getting into the car but halfway through, he paused. He then asked the attendant to wipe his windshield. For tipping the attendant, he went through the drill of taking out and replacing his wallet. Twice! Meanwhile, the longer queues at the other filling points had all dissipated like vapours of petrol. Any hope that I had had of reaching my meeting in time had also evaporated.

I sighed in an exaggerated manner and asked you again, my Lord—why have you blest me with such luck? I hope you will not consider me rude but just in case you have forgotten, I am yet to get a clear answer.

And Lord, have you ever seen my plight at the movies? It just has to be my luck that the romantic couple shall be seated right behind me. I often can't hear the on-screen dialogue because of the squeals and giggles of the feminine half of the couple. And the lover, sighing like a furnace, drowns every other sound.

If I buy popcorn during the intermission, I mostly get the hard kernels. And the misery is compounded by the uncle with the prostate problem who has to go past my seat to the washroom every half an hour. He steps on my toes on the way out, and again on the way in. Each and every time!

And Lord, don't give me any of those platitudes about why into each life some rain must fall. That is all nonsense because far too much has been falling in mine! Not just rain. Do you remember the time, Lord, when I wore my new suit to appear at that interview and something fell on my shoulder while I was passing under that tree on which you make so many birds sit? Remember when I had to participate in that debate and I got a sore throat? The time when I tripped getting on stage for that audition? Do I need to recall how my luck did not let me win the lottery by just one digit? Have you forgotten that time when that almost-full bottle of my favourite single malt slipped out of my hands?

Quite frankly, I have lost count of the number of times my bad luck has tested my patience beyond endurance.

But do I complain, O Lord, do I? No! And that is only because of the pleasure I derive by holding forth at parties about my awful luck and my trials and tribulations. But Lord, why is it that often there is some old bore at the party with a litany of complaints longer than mine? And he holds the audience in thrall, speaking in his childish treble, being almost sans teeth, sans eyes, sans everything! Surprisingly, it is he who gets everyone's sympathy!

And no one listens to me, O Lord! Why do I have to have all the bad luck? Why me, O Lord! Why me?

16
Selective Amnesia

Verily it has been said that he who wields the biggest stick shall claim the buffalo to be his own!

And thus, it is possible for a minister of the Union government to claim that he was so busy with his onerous duties that he forgot to file his income tax returns for a whole decade! And thus it is possible for sundry political, social or religious worthies to deny ever having said whatever stupid thing they did say—even when there are audio and video proofs of their indiscretions.

Because with authority comes shamelessness. With authority comes brazenness. With authority comes immunity. With the *lathi* comes the *bhains*! It is the one in authority who decides what to remember and what to forget. It is the one in power who decides in what form to remember that which is not to be forgotten. It is the winner who writes history. It is the victor who rewrites history!

Let the record show that I have explicated this great truth!

It is in keeping with this truth that the income tax officer remembers to impose a penalty on me for some trifling transgression, conveniently forgetting to sanction me that refund of overpaid tax which has now been due for the past five years.

It is in keeping with this truth that my bank selectively remembers to deduct tax at source on the paltry interest on my fixed deposits, conveniently forgetting that I have submitted Form Something 'A' and Declaration Umpteen IV (2), according to which no tax should be deducted.

It is in keeping with this truth that my cranky boss dredges up the one instance when I was late reaching office, conveniently forgetting that I have told him eleventeen times that due to heavy rain, parts of the city were flooded that day.

Oh, but the most outrageous wounds are inflicted by the slings and arrows flung by one's near and dear ones when they uphold this truth. Shakespeare said that. And if he did not, he should have.

It is in keeping with this truth that the little woman causes me the most grief. After all, who commands higher power than the high command? For me, the high, high command is my wife. Her imperious behaviour is the ultimate validation of my theory that selective amnesia is directly proportional to the power wielded by a person.

She has never let me forget that one time when I forgot one of our anniversaries. And it was not our wedding anniversary. It was the anniversary of our first time going out together for a cup of coffee. She celebrates many such anniversaries—the first time she used my credit card, the first time I ate *kaddu* cooked by her, the first time we were stranded on the highway because I had neglected to check the spare.

Oh yes! She celebrates many such anniversaries, and she does not let me forget them. But she conveniently forgets the many times that I have brought her flowers or chocolates. Even when it was not her birthday or an anniversary or I had done nothing wrong!

She will never ever let me forget the embarrassment of landing up at Paul's house for his wedding reception a day after the actual event. She conveniently disregards the fact that another time, we reached Peter's place for dinner a day early; on Saturday instead of Sunday. According to my arithmetic, a day late and a day early neatly cancel each other out. But for my soulmate? They are two different nails—to be hammered as many times as needed.

She will berate me and keep destroying my confidence in myself each time I have a drink (which is almost every day). She recalls that one incident of its kind, when we had shifted from part A of the town to part B. A week or so after the shift, we had met some friends at the club, and I had imbibed a generous quantity. It was late when my wife and I left for home, with me behind the wheel. We reached home but there was another car parked in the garage. It was only then that it struck me that we now lived in a house in part B of town. Muscle memory had made me drive to our old house in part A!

And she will never let me forget this incident.

I keep asking her why she had not pointed out that we were headed in the wrong direction. After all, she had not taken part in the drunken revelry. But her answer has always been the same.

'I have so much to do. Don't expect me to know the roads. In any case, that is your responsibility.'

So pray, what is hers? Surely not to cook because she forgets to use salt altogether at least once a week. When I timidly request her at the table to pass me the salt cellar, I am told to eat the dal as it is. She justifies it by saying that a low sodium intake is good for my health. I really admire her concern for my health. I more admire her ability to keep a straight face while eating that same dal without adding any salt, unless she does it so surreptitiously that I do not get to know. Be that as it may, the fact remains that she will never admit to any mistake on her part.

I would like the United Nations General Assembly or the Security Council or whoever does these kinds of things to take up a special motion to prescribe a sunset clause on the acts of omission and commission of a husband. I demand that a time limit be set, specifying in terms of days and years, within which a wife may dig up an old incident or grievance, real or imaginary, to unfairly exploit it in an entirely unrelated context.

I would like to highlight the need for this by recalling a really old incident. It must have been in 326 BC or AD 1066 or some other such forgettable year in which some crook picked my pocket outside the crowded Odeon theatre, where the little woman and I had gone to watch a movie.

The statement above is correct to the best of my knowledge and belief. To wit, that 'some crook picked my pocket.' But the lady has never let me forget that loss. As she says, that was 'the day I had let some crook pick my pocket.' When she is in a foul mood, she goes so far as to remember it as 'the day that I had had my pocket picked'—as if I were a conspirator and a collaborator!

The whole point of the story is that the tickets for the movie and all my money were in that very wallet. We had to return home without watching the movie. That too on foot!

Even today, aeons later, when I want to go out with my friends for a boisterous evening, the little woman smugly says, 'Go by all means, but remember the time you had had your pocket picked!'

A sensible reaction to such an illogical statement would be, 'For heaven's sake, woman! That happened ages ago and what does that have to do with going out with my friends tonight?'

But do I say it? No! Because I am the politest of husbands! And because the great truth is that it is for her to decide what to remember and what to forget.

Because it is she who wields the biggest stick—the buffalo belongs to her!

17

Decisions...Decisions!

My Guru used to say, 'Take a decision. Take a decision!' He always said that even a bad decision is better than no decision.

'If you make a bad decision, you can always change it later. But not taking a decision is debilitating. It shall sap your morale and cause depression. A decision is a leap of faith! Every decision has to be taken with incomplete knowledge. If you wait to collect all relevant information, you shall never take a decision. The trick is to err less and less. Remember, there is no such thing as a perfectly correct decision!'

Thus, for many happy years, I followed my Guru's advice. I blithely kept taking decisions—big and small. Without pausing for even a moment, I would happily buy the red shirt with scant regard for the fact that I had no trousers that could match that particular shade. I would buy the luminescent green coloured kurta and wear it with my brown-striped pyjamas.

I looked ridiculous. I always appeared to be dressed like a clown. But I couldn't care less. At least I was clothed.

I took equally quick and firm decisions regarding food. In a restaurant, I would order the dish listed at the top, accompanied by one dish listed in the middle of the main course. Sometimes the stuff was horrid, and sometimes it was worse. But it was a quick and efficient way to order a meal.

At home, my man Friday always asked what was to be cooked and I always decided quickly and firmly. Once a friend dropped in and I invited him to join me for lunch. He seemed surprised to be served two types of dals and nothing else. I had to let him know that when the man Friday had asked whether to cook dal A or B, I had told him to cook both. A quick and clean decision!

My reputation as a gourmet might not have been the greatest, but I never went hungry.

Early in my career, I had to move from one town to another. I never wasted time or effort on deciding the house or the locality in which to stay. I always made a quick and firm decision to take a house on rent. At one place, getting a good night's rest was quite difficult because the railway station was close by, and at another, the planes passing overhead were a bit of a nuisance. Notwithstanding these minor irritations, I could say with pride that I had a roof over my head.

Existing was a pleasure. Life had fixed points. Black was black. White was white. There were no grey areas. Everything was definite. Life was good and I saw no reason to improve it. I believe engineers are familiar with the dilemma of constantly trying to improve a design. The irony is that if a product is always under improvement, the gizmo is never available for use. Hence, engineers have the important concept of 'freezing the design'. At some point in time, a decision has to be taken that no further improvements shall be attempted so that the engineering marvel goes into production.

I had adopted this sensible principle of freezing the design as a philosophy for guiding myself from childhood to senility.

Life was good. Why try to improve it? 'Never tinker with perfection' was my proud motto. And in my opinion, I was perfect.

Then I decided to get married. Suddenly, I was plunged into a morass of indecision, doubt and vacillation. There were pitfalls everywhere. If I managed to avoid one trap, there were two other hazards waiting for me. Life became a rudderless boat in tempestuous seas. There were no fixed points. Nothing was certain. Even the most minor activity became susceptible to second guessing. The enormity of likely consequences demanded that even inconsequential decisions be examined for pros and cons, and then cons and pros once again. Every minor decision had to be put off till more information became available.

'What would you like to eat for lunch?'

'Let's have mutton!'

'But that's red meat! Cholesterol!'

'Okay, could we have chicken?'

'Are you crazy? Haven't you read about the conditions in which they are reared?'

'Fine, then fish it is! Lots of Omega-3 and whatnot, right?'

'And mercury!'

'Could we have some vegetables then? Potatoes? Cabbage?'

'Do you want to get fat? Haven't you heard about those beastly things that hide in cabbages?'

'Okay then. You decide, I shall eat whatever you cook.'

'Why can't I get even a simple decision out of you? Why must you dilly-dally so?'

It is not just our lunch that gets delayed. We seem to find a host of reasons for not taking a decision on any issue, big or small.

Last week, I needed a new razor. My soulmate wanted to ensure that I did not buy any of those cheap imitations. It had to be the genuine article and because we could not be certain, we did not buy any razor. I now have a three-day fuzz, but she will not let me buy any spurious product.

I guess I shall look quite the intellectual with a beard.

Our holiday to Switzerland last summer was cancelled because maybe it would have been too cold. Egypt was bound to be too hot and Thailand would have probably been too humid. We did not go to Angkor Wat because of Moulin Rouge (her words, not mine) and the Dead Sea remains off-limits because bombs are falling all over the place there, you see? We shall not be visiting Kandy either, because remnants of some Tigers might be lurking in the underbrush.

My true love and I need to buy a house. But property prices are always either going down or up or this way or that. We need a small house, but later we might need a big one because of the children. But the kids shall grow up and leave home and then we shall be saddled with too big a house. So who needs such a large house? In any case, we do not know the track record of the builder and next year property prices might dip.

I had been nonchalance personified till I got married. Within a couple of years of becoming a dear hubby, I became a dithering Hamlet!

I am now looking for my Guru—that guy who said that there is no such thing as a perfectly correct decision and that if you take a bad decision, you can always change it and take a fresh decision.

I have not found him yet, but when I do, I intend to ask him two questions. One: 'While you did tell me that there is no such thing as a perfectly correct decision, why didn't you tell me that it is possible to take a perfectly wrong decision?' And two: 'How do you go about undoing the decision to get married?'

18

Stamp Out the Past

The English have their attics and basements and cellars. The Swiss have their bank vaults and the Germans have their thick walls in which they hide heirlooms and family secrets. Their generations to come discover these gewgaws and doodahs and baubles, which are then declared by Sotheby's and Christie's to be priceless antiques! You must have read about them too: the hunk of emerald that was used as a doorstop for decades by an unaware family, the soot-covered idol which was a rare ninth-century metalwork, the shoddy diary that was the lost manuscript of the greatest of poets. You get the drift of what I am saying, don't you?

Well, in India we have no such thing. It is difficult, if not downright impossible, to refer to a cellar or an attic when you have lived in eleventy-two different houses in the span of thirty years, transferred by the powers that be from town A to B to C. Till one day, the powers that be run out of letters of the alphabet and suggest that you hang up your briefcase and your tiffin carrier while the going is still good.

During the years that you remained in service, the same powers that be indulged their warped sense of humour by housing you in a wide range of living quarters, from haunted bungalows with umpteen twelve-foot-high doorways to the embarrassing, almost shameful 'hostel' accommodation, comprising one room, a kitchenette and one seven-foot-high entrance.

My journey in the service of Bharat *sarkar* was no different and we moved to a house with a sense of settling down only after I retired. In the various earlier shifts between towns A and B and C, the standard practice had been to dump everything into cartons, packing cases, suitcases and trunks, with the promise to oneself that the detritus would be sorted out and organized in the new lodgings. Of course, that never came to pass.

It was only after the final shift that I paid attention to the desi equivalent of the attic/vault/cellar. As everyone knows, humble middle-class India carries from one place to another its very own attic slash vault slash cellar in the form of an oversized steel trunk, always a relic of some age gone by. This unwieldy trunk used to be an essential part of the bride's trousseau in any respectable family.

The large trunk that my wife brought with her when we got married remained her exclusive property and domain. She would ceremoniously have the trunk opened twice a year—once shortly after Diwali to take the quilts out and once shortly after Holi to pack them away, along with anything else not of immediate use. Both occasions would be marked by the ceremonious dunking of vast quantities of naphthalene balls into the trunk. My wife never allowed me near the trunk—her explanation being that the heavy lid would fall on my head! Why she was not scared of it falling on her own head has forever remained a mystery to me.

With my retirement, I have realized that an empty mind is not just the devil's workshop, it is also the abode of Thanatos—the god of self-destruction. The devil and Thanatos together goaded me to be indiscreet last week when the missus had gone for a day-long picnic with her kitty friends. I decided to open the steel trunk and take the gamble of having the heavy lid fall on my head.

Opening the huge steel trunk was akin to accessing a portal into the past. Besides the quilts and woollens, there were mothballs from last year, fairly large even now. Then there were mothballs of earlier times—each year showing a diminishing presence. I peered into one corner and could make out pinhead-sized pearls; mothballs from the last decade.

At the bottom of the steel trunk, there were a few old woollens, a couple of silver bowls, some dog-eared magazines, an oddly familiar-looking folder, and a file containing recipes snipped out from various publications. I took out the yellowing newspaper that lined the bottom of the steel trunk and I was taken aback to see that it was almost fifteen years old! I started reading the paper, yellowed and streaked with rust.

So much has changed! Yet so little!

I picked up the vaguely familiar folder. Hey! This was my stamp collection! My prized collection! I had not seen it maybe for the past twenty years, but I would recognize it anywhere. My precious collection of stamps from the world over!

Excitedly, I called out to my granddaughters. 'Hey, come here, you two!' I had to shout thrice before they peeled themselves away from the television set.

'What is it, Nana?' said the elder one, impatiently.

'What is it now, Nana?' said the younger one, petulantly.

'See! This is my stamp collection! I had the best stamp collection in my class,' I said proudly.

'What is a stamp?' said the younger one.

'What is a stamp collection?' asked the elder one.

'Stamps were used to send letters. There were special stamps for airmail and stickers for express delivery. There were postcards and inland letters and aerogrammes!'

The elder one looked at the younger one. The younger one looked at the elder one. Both rolled their eyes.

'Why would you need these things called stamps for sending letters? Why didn't you use email?'

'Well, we used to write letters on paper and then post them.'

'You mean you first typed your letter, then took a printout of the word file, scanned the hard copy and then posted a jpeg file on your home page? How stupid!' said the elder one.

'I have immigration stamps in my passport,' declared the younger one.

'No, no, not those stamps. These were stamps that we collected. When we had duplicates, we also exchanged them. I collected first-day covers and special issues and commemoratives. My pen friend from Sweden sent me many stamps, too.'

'Exchanged stamps?' The elder one was nonplussed.

'Pen friend? Is that something like a Facebook friend?' asked the younger one.

'Why don't you listen when I am telling you something?' said I.

The elder one looked at the younger one. The younger one looked at the elder one. Both rolled their eyes.

'We are sure you had a good time with those stamps, Nana,' said the elder one.

'As long as you enjoyed it,' said the younger one. Patronizingly.

'I would want you both to have my stamp collection after I am gone.'

'What shall we do with it? Where are you going to go?' asked the younger one.

'What is it good for? Why would anyone collect anything as stupid as stamps?' asked the elder one.

Whenever my granddaughters run out of adjectives, the 'S' word is spoken. Shoes that slip are stupid. Ice cream that melts is stupid. Pencils that break are stupid. Pizzas that are cold are stupid. Remote controls with worn-out batteries are stupid.

I went into a long explanation about the pleasures of a hobby and the educational value of collecting stamps. I waxed eloquent on the wonderful stamps from Hungary, the USSR, San Marino and Ceylon. I showed them the special stamps, the triangles, the diagonals and the se-tenants. I tried to explain terms like perforations, cancellations and hinges. I showed them the oldest stamps in my collection and made them read out the names of the issuing countries.

The elder one looked at the younger one. The younger one looked at the elder one. Both rolled their eyes.

'Nana, you can't fool us. You can't make up names of countries! Whoever heard of Magyar Posta? Helvetia! Ha ha! That's a good one! And look at this. Kenya-Uganda-Tanganyika! Nana, someone really fooled you. There are no countries with names such as Ceylon, CCCP or Czechoslovakia!'

Crestfallen, I tried to change the subject.

'We also collected matchbook covers. I had a good collection of coins. Some of my friends collected cigarette packets. We used to cut them in rings to make paper chains. We also made cups and glasses and peashooter pellets out of the aluminium foil from inside the empty cigarette packs.'

The elder one was horrified. 'How could your parents be

so irresponsible? Collecting cigarette packets! Indeed!'

'I like collecting coins. But I like collecting currency notes better,' said the younger one, primly. 'Why don't you give me a few notes to add to my collection?'

I tried to take control of the conversation. 'You girls should understand that there is a world larger than your tablets and smartphones and television sets!'

'Mommmeeee!' screamed the elder one in her shrill voice. 'Nana is again telling us his weird old-time stories. We aren't stupid. Why does he expect us to believe him?'

'Nana is not letting us do our stupid homework,' screamed the younger one.

'Daddyeee!' screamed my daughter from the kitchen. 'Why do you keep hassling them? Let them watch the stupid TV!'

'Beta, but I am only trying to...' I ended, lamely.

'Well, whatever it is, don't do it!' screamed my daughter, still in the kitchen.

It was with some difficulty that I opened the large steel trunk. Then without any regret, I dumped the stamp album in it. As I closed the trunk, the lid slipped and hit me on the head.

'Stupid trunk!' I muttered.

19
The Bitter Half

My wife and I are supreme intellectuals. With little provocation and no excuse whatsoever, we enter into complicated discussions on non-existential issues. We talk of many things; of shoes and ships and sealing wax, of cabbages and kings, and why I am fat and beer in packs, and wholly asinine stuff like that.

Just this evening, we were discussing the manner in which the government goes about wasting the money that I pay as tax.

'You know,' I said to the better half conversationally. 'It used to be fashionable to talk of levying expenditure tax in place of income tax. It was touted as the answer to black money.

'But with this Jee-Ess-Tee thing, I suffer a double whammy! I pay income tax as well as expenditure tax. I part with almost half my income! And the government squanders it on freebies and for building castles in the air! Why can't I too splurge the remaining amount in a foolish manner?' I asked.

'Because, stupid, it's the only money left with us! If you spend that also foolishly, what shall we live on? As it is, you waste enough.'

It was on this bank and shoal of time that the discussion between yours truly and the better half entered a dangerous territory.

'What...!!!'

'Yes! And don't you dare waste more.' For good measure, so that I was not left in any doubt, the wife added, 'Just because I am so tolerant, doesn't mean that you can go around squandering money as if you are a political leader!'

'What... Who... How?' I sputtered. 'Have I ever wasted money? I am so, so thrifty! How is it even possible for you to think that I waste money?'

Everyone knows that government expenditure is audited after the money has evaporated, or leaked or transmogrified into coffers known, unknown or located in Switzerland. This is not the case with my expenses. They are subjected to preaudit (Why do you need three thousand rupees for a bottle of whisky?), current audit (Why do you need a bottle of whisky when you already have a half-full one on the sideboard?), and postaudit (How could you have finished the bottle so quickly?)

The audit by the better half is thorough and has a 360-degree perspective. No one questions government expenditure, but my wife poses questions that are difficult, if not impossible, to answer.

'Why is the cost of a bottle more than last year?'

'Does your friend Rishabh spend as much on liquor?'

'Why can't you buy a cheaper brand of whisky?'

'In college, you always shared a coke with me to save money. Why do you now need a whole bottle of whisky all for yourself?'

'But...but...but...'

'Admit it. You fritter away so much! You keep buying a whole lot of stuff that you never use.'

After many such confrontations, I have learnt that an attack can only be thwarted by launching a counterattack.

So I decided to take the offensive. Foolishly.

'Look who is calling the pot black!' I shouted. 'What about you? You bought those gold bangles last Diwali; but have you ever worn them? No sirree! They have been lying in the bank locker for the past many months.'

'Yes! And whose fault is that?' asked the wife. 'It is so dangerous to go out wearing expensive jewellery!'

So, all of a sudden, the bad law-and-order situation is because of some act of omission or commission on my part?

Pushed into this desperate situation, I needed to open another front. 'What about that expensive silk sari that you bought in Kanchipuram when we visited there more than twenty years ago? You haven't worn it even once!'

'I bought it especially for wearing at my friend Sarita's wedding. When she gets married, I will wear it.'

Considering that her friend Sarita is now fifty years or more, I doubt if that particular sari will ever come out of the wardrobe. But did I have the guts to say so? Did I have the gumption? Even as I tried to think of a response that was both devastating and guaranteed to not add fuel to the fire, a fresh salvo was fired.

'It is you who keeps throwing away money on useless schemes and things'.

I panicked! I thought that the better half had got to know about the mutual fund in which I had invested substantial amounts, and which had gone belly up last Friday. But her target was something more tangible.

'Just look at that fire extinguisher! You bought it ten years ago. And you haven't used it even once. And you throw good money after bad by getting it checked and refilled every year!'

'But…but…' was all I managed to say before she hurled another accusation.

'You bought that hockey stick and you don't even play hockey!'

'Well, dear, a hockey stick is so convenient. Just suppose I want to shoo a stray dog away?'

'Oh, puh-leeze!' sneered the wife. 'The last time there was a cat in the kitchen, you ran and hid under the bed!'

'That is so not true!' I hotly contested the slander. 'I was searching for the hockey stick, which I thought you had put away under the bed. You do tend to hide things away, don't you?'

'Now don't change the subject,' she said. 'The fact remains that you don't play hockey and you have never used it to scare away an insect, let alone a big bad kitten.'

'Look, my dear, I need that hockey stick for self-defence. I need to have a weapon handy in case there is a burglar lurking in the shadows. I shall hit him for a six, the way I used to hook a bouncer when I played cricket!'

'But you might kill the poor fellow!' exclaimed the better half. I could not make out if this was said sarcastically.

'You wait and see. I will hit him for a six.'

'Ha ha! I think you shall never get to use your precious hockey stick. It will prove to be useless, just like that spare tyre that you keep in the car.'

'But listen, darling. Every car needs a spare. Just in case…'

'Just in case!' she sneered. 'Just like the health insurance you buy each time you travel abroad, which you haven't used even once!'

'But look here…' I started to argue.

'You are so easy to fool! Take that scoundrel, your

insurancewallah! He came to collect your cheque for the car insurance, and he sold you insurance for the house. Do you have any idea how much money you have paid, year after year, and there has not been a single claim?'

'What do you want me to do?' I exploded. 'Do you want me to arrange for a flood or a fire or an earthquake?'

'You don't have to! But you can stop wasting money!'

'That is not a waste,' I contested hotly. 'It is essential. Just in case.'

'Oh, I understand your "just in case"! You squander money and keep using your "just in case" as an excuse.'

'But...but...' I fulminated.

'No "buts" about it! Look at that hurricane lamp. You had gone to buy some inverter system so that we need not sit in the dark when there is a power breakdown. And what did you get? That damn hurricane lamp, which you have not used even once!'

'But that is because there have been no power failures,' I protested.

'Of course there have been! One time you fumbled around for ten minutes, searching for a matchbox. And the last time, you declared that the lamp had no kerosene oil!'

'Yes! And why did the hurricane lamp have no kerosene oil? Because only poor people are allowed to buy kerosene oil! We can't because we are above the poverty line!' I declared proudly.

The lights went out just then, leaving us in the gathering darkness. My wife stormed out of the house in disgust and drove away in anger.

I do not know where she has gone, but she will return after she cools off. Unless there is a puncture—because she doesn't know how to change a tyre!

Meanwhile I sit here, in almost total darkness, surrounded by many of my worldly possessions which my wife accuses me of having wasted money on. One fire extinguisher. Many health insurance policies for foreign travel which are now reduced to waste paper. A hockey stick thirsting for some burglar blood. A hurricane lamp that shall never be lit.

And as I sit here, sipping my expensive whisky, I keep wondering why the better half is called the better half and why the husband should not be called the bitter half.

20

If Only the Twain Could Meet

My mind and my body have been living together for more than seventy years. But, like the superpowers at the height of the Cold War, the two never see eye to eye. They seldom agree on any issue and have divergent approaches to most subjects. Their most vehement disagreements are on schedules.

When my mind is fully awake, my body wants to sleep. And when my body is fully awake, my mind goes to sleep.

This is not a new affliction. Throughout the many years that I have had to sit through lectures, seminars, meetings, conferences and discussions, I have rarely been able to get my mind and body to pay attention at the same time.

Little wonder that my teachers in school used to call me 'the zombie'. I came to be known as the 'sleeping beauty' in college because I insisted that my classmates were not to disturb my sleep. They were, however, to nudge me awake if I started snoring or the professor asked me a direct question. The arrangement worked fine for a long time, but one day the friend who was to act as sentry also fell asleep. As a result, both of us were banished from Professor Trikha's classes forever.

It also came to pass in the fullness of time that my colleagues in office dubbed me the 'snoring wonder'. I was notorious for falling asleep in meetings, presentations and even during lunch breaks. There were many colleagues who were more than familiar with my 'body awake, mind asleep' avatar and laid bets on how long it would be before the boss addressing us would realize that though I sat up straight, my mind was asleep.

This continued till I myself became senior enough to chair meetings and committees and whatnots. This did not pose a great problem because I had mastered the art of letting my mind sleep while the wide-awake body sat erect. A carelessly worded question at the end usually sufficed to convince junior officers that I had listened to them with rapt attention. In fact, all the bilge being dished out by them never entered my ears!

Actually, my mind comes into its own after midnight, when the limbs start weighing a ton and the eyes start getting glassy. It is then that the mind lights up with paradigm-changing ideas and literary gems that would undoubtedly endure for generations, if only they were recorded. But the body is sleepy, so the mind grudgingly agrees to wait till morning to put that brainwave on paper. After all, it is so vividly etched in the mind that it can definitely wait till the morn. Who knows, the idea might even get refined once I have slept on it?

Alas and alack! In the morning—poof! There is not even a smidgeon of soot to show where that brilliant idea got incinerated.

Let me proclaim that it is not just once in a blue moon that these insights flash like lightning in my wide-awake mind. In fact, these brilliant flashes occur quite frequently. If only I could remember the idea I had on Monday night, I would have solved the problem of want in this world. The idea on Tuesday night would have brought everlasting peace. The idea on Wednesday would have ensured salvation for all of humanity!

The only hitch is that when I wake up, I can never recall details of those light-bulb moments. My long-suffering wife has got quite used to my looking like a lost puppy in the morning, as I try to piece together the shreds of the forgotten grand design.

Things would have continued forever in this disorganized way, but last month my wife read somewhere that some tailor named Coleridge wrote his best stuff when he was asleep. So she ordered me to work for my Nobel in literature by keeping a notepad by the bedside. Her instructions were clear: I was to force my sleepy body to do the bidding of a wide-awake mind. I too welcomed the prospect of jotting down all the magic stuff that crowds my mind when the body is asleep.

The first night I had a brainwave, but I could not remember what it was about. The second night, I made a superhuman effort and as instructed by my wife, wrote down all the thoughts that I had regarding some very important matter. There was nothing on the pad in the morning. The pen had no ink!

After a few more misses, one morning I got up with the certainty that during the night I had made a note of all solutions to global concerns. I eagerly picked up the notepad.

Oh, how horrible! During the night, someone had scribbled a lot of illegible stuff in my notepad. I write in a bold cursive, and the page before my eyes was covered with spidery scrawls. But considering that no one else could have entered the bedroom, I had to accept that whatever was recorded was my very own effort. And what was recorded seemed to make no sense at all! The only words that were legible seemed to be:

'If you peel an orange.' That was all! 'If you peel an orange.'

One can see that the possibilities are endless; but, by itself, the statement 'If you peel an orange.' does not really solve many problems. Nor is it great literature. I toyed a bit with the statement. Would it make more sense if the statement had a comma instead of a period at the end?

I gave up. A profound statement such as this could be interpreted only by great minds and only after the passage of a sufficient period of time.

In the narration above, it is possible that I have been swayed by the hyperbole of my own rhetoric. The statement that my mind and body are never on the same wavelength might be an exaggeration. I have to confess that my mind and body are, in fact, in perfect synchronization for about three hours every day. The two are never awake at the same time but both do enter into a profoundly deep sleep at the same time. This is the part of the day immediately after sunrise. As a result, in the summer months, I wake up at around eight in the morning. A little bit of calculation would reveal that my waking up time in the winter months is around ten, ante meridiem.

One of these days, my mind and body shall learn to work in unison. Imagine where the world would have been if the USSR and the USA had worked in tandem after the Second World War! Comparable benefits for the world are guaranteed the day my mind and body pull in the same direction, at the same time. The opportunity that the human race lost because of the cussedness of the superpowers shall now be made good by me. It is I who will ensure phenomenal advances in science, literature, medicine and space technology—just as soon as I succeed in getting my mind and body to be awake at the same time. The world has no option but to wait.

21

The Wise Guy

Why is it that every desi becomes wise after going to *Amreeka?*

There is this guy who was in college with me. He was an average *kaddu*, just like me. He and I spent many years in the college café, without allowing any kind of wisdom to come anywhere near us. No one could have ever accused us of being intellectuals.

And this guy returns from Amreeka with lots of *gyan* and suggests we meet in the cafe for old times' sake. And he keeps spouting gyan for hours on end! He really goes at me—hammer and tongs—without once revealing why he is so cheesed off with his homeland.

'Every sovereign nation prides itself on its sense of nationhood,' says Giani. 'The territorial integrity, constitution, language, religion, culture and history of the people define the nation and the people. Every nation prides itself on its symbols of nationhood.'

So far, I have no dispute. What is the point that my desi bhai is driving at?

'Of course, you are right. And we have all those things in ample measure and more in India, that is, Bharat. We are a proud nation,' I declare.

'Yes, but look at what you have done to each and every

one of your symbols of national pride! You have managed to ruin everything!

'On my flight from the Yew-Ess, I learnt that Air India, your so-called flag carrier, has been hived off. And your currency! I could not believe my eyes when I exchanged dollars at the airport.'

Yes, I admit that we are not yet as familiar with the new currency notes as we were with the old ones. Equally, there are some facets of the new currency notes that are best left unmentioned. Hardly anyone could have forgotten one of the senior-most mandarins of the North Block declaring that the new two-thousand-rupee note was genuine only if the colour bled! Even as I was wondering whether Giani had heard that story, he whipped out two dissimilar five hundred rupees notes from his wallet.

'Whaddya know,' he said in a faux Yankee drawl. 'Both these babies are genuine! How can you have dissimilar currency notes and declare all variants to be genuine?

'And look at your coins! The one-rupee and two-rupee coins circulate in all eighty-four lakh patterns and sizes. The five-rupee coins are available in as many variations. The ten-rupee coins are also available in dissimilar versions. And your Reserve Bank of India has declared that all are legal tender!'

Now I can argue as well as any other ill-informed guy, so l held my own against the bigoted views of Giani. I tried to convince him that there is no nation better or prouder of its coinage, its heritage, its history and its geography than we are in this great country of India, that is, Bharat.

But Giani attacked on a new front now. 'Look at your stamps! Once in a while I get a letter by post from India. I must say that most of your common stamps are a shame. And your Department of Posts has been pushed out of business by private courier companies. It seems to be surviving on banking operations and by selling dal!'

I kept quiet. I just did not want Giani to rake up the other shameful stamp issue, the private enterprise of Telgi. But Giani was relentless.

'Do you remember how Telgi privatized the printing of stamp papers?'

I cringed. Nonetheless, I hotly contested the assertion.

I did not know what hurt more—Giani recalling these issues or his constantly distancing himself by referring to his motherland as 'your country'. But Giani was really in form, and getting more vociferous by the minute. So much so that many others in the café were now following our discussion.

'Your armed forces and the civil bureaucracy have been taking potshots at each other, reducing the stature of both. Your judiciary has enough enemies, but it seems it does not need them! It has been steadily sinking under the weight of its own pomposity and incompetence. I find your media to be a joke! In public life, the statesmen of yore are gone, as are even the leaders of the nation and men. You are left with a ragtag bunch of politicians and hooligans. They do little but indulge in competitive mud-slinging and anticipatory sycophancy!'

'Hey, now wait a minute,' I shouted. 'That is so unfair and ill-informed!'

Others in the café were now wondering whether the two of us would come to blows. As a matter of abundant precaution, one waiter surreptitiously removed the knives and forks from our table.

'You know,' continued Giani, 'in just the few days that I

have been back, I could not help noticing that all the icons of yesteryears have been exhumed from history and pilloried in ever-changing contexts. Each wart, each misdemeanour, each failing has been magnified to reduce the stature of every towering figure. All reputations seem to have been blown to smithereens. Every national leader one can think of has been besmirched or mired in some controversy—real or fabricated. National icons have been dragged down and in the dust, made humble with the poor *syce* and slave!'

'Your *angrezi* has improved in Amreeka,' I said to Giani, trying to interrupt his flow.

'Have you ever watched the vulgar manner in which even your television channels lampoon your leaders?'

'You see, ours is a free country. We have our Constitution! It gives us so many rights. It ensures us freedom of expression and speech! We are proud of our freedom of speech!' I said. Not so much with conviction as by way of explanation.

'And yet you have problems with the publication of books and screening of films! Ha ha!'

'You see, we take the rights as enshrined in our Constitution very seriously.'

'What about your fundamental duties? They are in your Constitution too,' said my friend.

Well, I almost walked into that one! But just in time, I remembered that the Constitution does have some provision that enumerates the fundamental duties of citizens.

'Ah ha!' said I, 'but they are not mandatory!'

Giani said, 'That is just your problem! You will not do something unless you are forced to do it!'

There was no point in arguing with my videshi friend. He had obviously been brainwashed by the decadent West into condemning everything about his homeland. I, therefore, decided to extol the virtues of our most obvious icons, our national flag and the national anthem.

'Do you know,' said I, 'we have the most beautifully designed national flag. It has a pleasing colour scheme and a simple yet attractive design.'

Giani was in a foul mood. He said, 'Yet an industrialist had to go to court to get the right to fly it?'

And then surprisingly, my desi bhai sprang a surprise on me. I thought he was spouting superficial gyan but, surprise! Surprise! The guy had actually done some homework.

He said, 'You know, your national flag is supposed to "represent the hopes and aspirations of the people" and it has to be displayed keeping in mind "The Prevention of Insults to National Honour Act, 1971" as well as the instructions contained in the Flag Code of India 2002.

'Are you aware that your Flag Code contains elaborate instructions, down to ridiculous details? Do you know it says that when the national flag is hoisted in a school, the classes have to be arranged in order of seniority with a distance of at least one pace between two rows? Stupid! Have you ever wondered whether the principal of the school shall be liable for three years imprisonment if he stands four steps away from the flag post, instead of three as prescribed in the Flag Code? What happens when your flag is not made of khadi or khadi silk? Does the offender get three years?

'Hello! In the Yew-Ess we would ask, "Are you for real, man?"

'Do you know, instead of celebrating your national flag, you have created an obstacle course?'

'Well,' I started lamely. 'There must have been a good

reason if these stipulations have been made in the Flag Code.'

My friend Giani continued, 'You have managed to trivialize your national anthem. Some of your countrymen refuse to sing it because it has the word "Sindh" in it. Others cite religion as an excuse. Do you need your Supreme Court to tell you how to honour your anthem? Or how to do anything and everything? No wonder you are left with nothing to be proud of!'

I thought Giani had exceeded the bounds of decency but just to set the record straight, I said, 'Look, my friend, you are mistaken. We have so much to be proud of! We have Bollywood! We have cricket! We have our cricketing icons to be proud of.'

'Oh yes! That you do. But only till the next betting scandal hits the headlines!'

This was positively the last straw! There is just so much nonsense that can be tolerated against our great country! So, I decided to defend the honour of our motherland and gave Giani a resounding slap. Then I and some waiters threw Giani out of the café. It was most satisfying—the way everyone in the café sprang forward to perform their patriotic duty and started chanting:

'*Amreeka Hai! Hai!*'
'Giani Go Back!'
'*Amreeka Hai! Hai!*'
'Giani Go Back!'

22
And They Lived Happily Ever After

I have formulated a momentous theory—the Theory of Domestic Discord—which postulates that Indian households where womenfolk watch Hindi drama serials on television witness more bickering at bedtime. It is the interminable serials that cultivate a righteous sense of petulance among the ladies, giving rise to domestic strife. My theory may or may not be universally applicable, but empirical data of one household available to me validates the hypothesis. I know this because my missus subsists on a staple of those mopey, dopey serials. And thus it comes to pass almost every day that, just as the missus and I prepare to retire, we discover yet another issue to argue about and exchange unpleasantries.

The only respite is on Sundays when the wife's favourite serials are replaced by some other equally asinine programmes that she never watches. It is on Sunday evenings that I get to watch a rerun of some old movie or highlights of a game I missed during the week. Consequently, relative peace prevails without the usual arguments. Sometimes though, instead of the usual arguments, we have unusual ones!

Last Sunday, I resigned myself to spending a dull evening flipping through television channels from one silly programme to another. The old girl was babbling away about something. 'Aren't you listening? I said let us do something romantic for a change. Let us watch a movie together!'

'Oh no,' I groaned inwardly. This was not the time for the little woman to start acting out some juvenile fantasy. 'But I don't want to go out!' I declared irritably.

'Who said anything about going out? Do you think I am going to put makeup on again after washing my face? No way! No, we will watch some movie on Getflicks or Grime Video or something. But first, let me use the bathroom and get my turmeric milk.' While she was gone, I poured myself a generous shot of Remy Martin. She returned soon, fluffed up the pillows, and we settled down, propped up by countless pillows and cushions that the little woman insists on piling up in bed in unreasonably large numbers.

Just as I leaned back with a sigh, she asked, 'Have you locked the front door?'

I got up, made certain that I had indeed locked the door, and climbed back into bed. 'Did you check the gate?'

This time I unlocked the front door, walked the short driveway and assured myself that the gate had indeed been latched. I then locked the front door behind me and lugubriously got back into bed.

'You forgot to bring the remote,' she said. I got out of bed once more and fetched the remote control, but it stubbornly refused to work.

'The batteries have run down, silly. Didn't I tell you yesterday to change them?'

Off I went to the study to get fresh batteries. By the time I replaced the batteries in the remote and climbed back into bed, the missus needed to go to the bathroom once more.

She returned, but immediately she remembered that she had not applied her night cream. Every husband knows that this can take up to ten minutes with gentle massaging of the cheeks with fingertips, rolling of the earlobes between thumb and forefinger and long upward strokes of the palm on the neck, after which she needed to brush her hair again. Did I tell you that she believes in the old dictum of one hundred strokes of the brush before bed? Well, she does.

I waited, but lost patience at the count of forty-six or forty-seven and went to my small bar to pour another Remy. A larger one this time.

When I got back to the bedroom, she remembered that the milk that she had boiled would have cooled enough to be put away in the fridge. She returned after an eternity, by which time I was half asleep. She switched on something and Getflicks came on.

'What is my login ID?' she demanded.

I told her that her account probably expected her to log in with her email ID.

'Well, what is it?' she asked querulously. I told her her email ID.

'What is my password?' she asked.

'I don't know,' said I innocently, not daring to point out that I could not be expected to know a password set by her.

'How is it that you know my email ID but don't know the password?'

I let that pass and sarcastically said, 'Try 1234.'

'Hey, it worked!' she chortled. 'Why did you say you did not know the password?' I maintained a studied silence. I rightly believe that being right does not necessarily mean you have the right to state that you are right.

'Which movie do you want to watch?' By now, I was fully awake. 'Let us watch some thriller or some art film,' I said.

'But I want to watch a "boy meets girl" movie,' she said with stars in her eyes.

I did not see the light in her eyes and suggested instead that we watch some highbrow stuff. 'Let us watch *Ankur*. It is a Shyam Benegal classic, you know. You will love it!' I exclaimed.

She said firmly, 'Boy meets girl.'

There was a time when I could well have been accused of being naive as well as sentimental. But that was when I was stupider than stupid and could not hear what a girl was not saying. At that age, the fool that I was, I would have insisted on watching *Ankur*. Now, far wiser, I readily agreed to watch some tearjerker with the wholly predictable plot of Prince Charming riding off into the sunset with the lovely princess.

She selected a film and as soon as it started playing, she dozed off. After a while, I switched the television off and closed my eyes.

'How did it end?' she asked me in the morning.

'How did it end? I can't even recall how it started!'

'We must watch it again tonight,' she declared. I was indeed taken aback that the little woman was willing to forego her staple drama serial that evening.

So, on Monday night, we went through the whole process again. With the experience of Sunday behind us, we were able to accomplish the business of milk-turmeric-latch-gate-lock-door-night-cream-hundred-strokes-of-the-brush-two-Remy-Martins, etc., in double quick time.

'Let the movie start!' I declared grandly.

'What was the name of the one we were watching?' the

little woman asked. I could not recall the title. Nor could she. She started browsing through the menu until she came to a name that seemed familiar. 'This must have been the one,' she said.

The movie started, but no part of it seemed familiar. But the little woman seemed happy enough, so I said nothing. It appeared to be a boy-meets-girl story and there was nothing more to wish for. She sipped her turmeric milk. I sipped my Remy. The actors in the movie droned on. My Remy finished and I briefly contemplated getting up to get a refill. But it seemed too much of an effort. The actors still droned on.

Suddenly it was morning. The missus was fast asleep and so must have been I. Drowsily, I got up and switched off the television set that was still muttering away and went to the kitchen to make tea. Soon, I brought the steaming cups to the bedroom. By then, my wife was sitting up in bed, looking very pleased with herself.

'So, how did it end?'

'Oh, they lived happily ever after,' I took a guess.

'Isn't that so nice! We must do this more often,' she said.

I am left wondering what she meant—that we must watch movies together more often or that we should fall asleep without the usual bickering at bedtime more often? I guess if one wants to live happily ever after, one must not wonder too much.

23

Tied in Knots

My father had a term that was used with disdain for anyone who violated an unwritten dress code. The term was 'loafer'! Any person who wore a shirt other than a well-ironed white one was a loafer. Anyone carrying a handkerchief that was not white was a loafer. Anyone with long hair was a loafer. Anyone who had an unshaven look was a loafer. Any person who did not wear lace-up shoes was a loafer. Oxfords were mandatory, but derbies and brogues were alright too. However, loafers were meant for loafers! If anyone argued that pumps were fine at a black-tie event, I would have bet my money on that poor soul being dubbed a bounder by my father!

These days, I often look sadly at my paunch as I slip into my comfortable loafers. Wearing formal shoes is out of question because I can no longer bend down enough to tie the laces. But each time I slip on my lace-less shoes, I can hear my father's stentorian voice: 'Only loafers wear loafers!'

While my dad had strict views on shoes, shirts, handkerchiefs and just about everything else, his views on the protocol regarding ties were absolute and uncompromising. Anyone who wore a jacket without a tie was a loafer! And the tie had to be knotted just so! It had to be a Windsor knot or a four-in-hand, not some vulgar knot like an Eldredge or a Trinity! The single knot was also a no-no! It indicated an irresponsible approach to life and a propensity to be casual. Anyone who used the single knot was immediately classified as immature and unworthy of trust. While this was not as damning as being dubbed a loafer, it was not high praise either!

I do not think my old man was in a minority to hold this belief. Just about everyone in those days considered it unthinkable to wear a jacket of any sort sans a tie. Of course, the fops wore a bow with their smoking jackets and the more outdoorsy kind argued that a tie was not de rigueur with a hunting jacket. But for everyone else—the common people— an open collar was unthinkable while wearing a jacket.

The only exception—and my father heartily approved of it—was a sporty blazer, which could be worn even over a tee (Fred Perry; white). One was still encouraged to wear a scarf (white; silk or wool) with their blazers (navy blue; preferably serge). It needs to be recorded here in passing that the effete cravat and fancy ways of wearing it were largely unknown when I was young.

Because I was pummelled by such strong influences in my impressionable youth, I confess I have a somewhat ambivalent attitude towards the tie. When I am forced to wear this narrow sartorial accessory, I feel an overwhelming choking sensation. On the other hand, it helps to hide my bulging Adam's apple! I have also noticed that when I wear a jacket and tie, the fairer sex seems to find me irresistible. But when I sport an open collar, hardly anyone notices me, and no one gives that 'come hither' smile!

Just recently, I have decided to rise in revolt against the tie. While not exactly adopting a Bohemian lifestyle, I have switched to the laid-back jeans, khadi kurtas and chappals. I can afford to do so, being a stay-at-home author.

Even then, my heart bleeds for my countrymen who are not so fortunate! Not just for my countrymen, but many others in tropical climes who have to suffer this curse. It was those colonizers from clammy England who let loose this pestilence on the carefree populations in different parts of the world. And the tyranny of the vestigial tie in the form of the tie continues in many dominions of Her Majesty, even though the Sun set years ago on the empire.

The Sri Lankans were probably the smartest. They threw off the yoke by the cunning expedient of inventing the collarless dress shirt. This has considerably improved their quality of life. Serendipitously, it has also improved their cricket! Anyone who does not believe this only needs to recall what cricketing underdogs the Sri Lankans were, till their maverick performance in the World Cup of 1996!

The victory of the Bermudans has been much greater, yet lesser. They have managed to take their trousers off! But even as they have started wearing shorts, they could not shuck off the jacket or lose the noose. They now wear Bermudas to the beach without shirts and Bermudas to board meetings with shirts, jackets and ties!

I once suggested to a friend from Bermuda that in order to be truly liberated, they should have burnt the tie rather than their trousers. But he was quite clear in his mind, 'Oh thank you for your concern. Given the choice, we would like to continue with this arrangement. Don't you know it is better to be hot under the collar than under the belt?'

But just think! If they had had the gumption to shed the tie and jacket in addition to their trousers, how relaxed a civilization theirs would have been!

The Bermudans should inspire us to maintain our cool, at least under the belt. It is time that we Indians considered wearing a jacket and tie with the dhoti! It is not as if this has not been done. The uncommon man of R.K. Laxman wore a checked *bandhgala* with dhoti as long as he lived. Many a Munimji of the black-and-white movies also wore a coat (without a tie) and dhoti with aplomb. Why should we not?

To be fair, we have tried to escape the stranglehold of the necktie. The journey has been convoluted and marked by nebulous achievements. There was a time when the dress order 'formal' meant the black bandhgala and no other dress. 'Informal' attire meant a lounge suit (with a tie of course). Informal did not mean a tweed jacket with a tie, and definitely not any ethnic wear, no matter how chic.

To get over the formal-informal conundrum, we invented the dress code called casual. Casual meant any formal clothes but no tie. A course correction had to be applied when people started interpreting casual to mean jeans and tees, so casual was rechristened 'smart casual' and the term 'casual' came to be used for casual casual.

We have gradually invented several other dress codes to get around the stipulation of wearing a tie. Some of these do, in fact, require a tie to be worn but the overall effort is to wear clothes that are comfortable in our tropical climate. And the range of dress stipulations is truly impressive. Black tie, black tie optional, boardroom attire, business casual, business formal, casual, cocktail attire, cocktail attire festive, combination, come-as-you-please, formal, informal, jacket and tie, national dress, semi-formal, shirt and tie, smart casual and TGIF casuals.

Many of these are susceptible to delicious ambiguity. If I consult fashion gurus, I am bound to get conflicting advice. One might suggest that 'cocktail attire festive' means I should wear red socks, another might tell me to wear a black shirt. No matter what I wear, I shall not be right.

But I look at the bright side! If I can never be right, I can never be wrong either!

So, we have arrived at a stage where all dress codes are susceptible to considerable interpretational inexactitude. This gives the license to everyone to wear what they please, and the vast range of interpretations can be seen at any party or meeting, with pyjama kurtas rubbing, so to say, shoulder pads with tuxedos!

It is evident that while we have not been able to screw our courage to the sticking point, there is hope yet! We have not dared to discard the tie altogether, but we have been successful in finding ways to get around it. What a delightfully Indian solution!

24

Répondez S'il Vous Plaît

'Take the next turn and loop around once more,' I said to the driver.

'Why the hell did you have to hassle me to get ready quickly if all you wanted to do was to drive around aimlessly in the Delhi smog?' asked my darling wife, petulantly.

'Well, how was I to know that traffic would be so light today! We have been invited at eight and it is only seven fifty,' said I.

A while later, she asked, 'Okay, so now it is eight. Why don't we drive in, instead of waiting at this gate?'

'Wait a bit,' said I. 'We shall go in at five minutes past eight, rather than on the dot. If we march in on the dot, our host will think that I am a slave to the wristwatch.'

My darling merely rolled her eyes in the most exaggerated manner. I really do not know what she wants to convey when she behaves in this fashion, but do I create a scene? No, never!

I had half a mind to educate her on the huge difference between being late and being fashionably late for a party, but I let it be. My darling had already rung the bell and the explanation would need a wee bit more time. Maybe some other day.

Our hostess flung the door open—in a housecoat, her hair in curlers, and with a mudpack on her face! She was obviously expecting the unpunctual maid, who strolled in right behind us.

With a shriek, our hostess ran to some inner sanctum and it was left to the delinquent maid to invite us in and ask us to make ourselves comfortable.

We did.

I pointedly looked at my watch, which showed that it was twelve minutes past the appointed hour of eight.

'I say, we were asked to come at eight, weren't we?' I asked in an unnecessarily loud voice.

'Shush,' said my darling, and I shushed.

We must have waited an eternity for the other guests to arrive and by the time the cocktails were served, I was hungry. We had been there for another thousand hours, and I was sleepy, yet dinner was nowhere in sight. So we decided to go home. Without dinner. A few guests were still ambling in at about eleven when we were leaving.

And that has been the story of my life.

It is not uncommon for me to drive like a fiend to reach some rendezvous at the stipulated 8 p.m. or whatever, only to discover that I could have easily arrived an hour later and still no one would have noticed!

Just last week, we were caught in two traffic jams on the way to my friend Gupta's house and I really had to use all my skills to drive fast. Two careless trucks grazed past us quite dangerously and a cyclist tried to knock us over. Still, I managed to screech to a halt at Gupta's door at 8.35 p.m. Gupta had asked us to come at 8.30 and my driving skills had saved the day once again!

But Gupta had not yet returned from his office and Mrs Gupta was busy supervising the catering staff. It sure seemed as if it would be a big party. And a very long evening.

My darling and I waited in the totally deserted drawing room of the Gupta mansion.

'See,' I said with undisguised glee. 'We reached in time!'

'Yes,' said my darling in her resigned voice—the voice she reserves for me when I have tested her patience beyond endurance. 'We are early yet again.'

'No, darling, I beg to differ,' I said. 'We are again on time. Everyone else is late again!'

'That is all very well,' said my darling. 'But did you notice the scowl on Mrs Gupta's face?'

This whole business of throwing a party and attending one is a fairly straightforward matter. But people complicate issues and try to make it a sociological puzzle. It only proves that the whole world is increasingly out of sync with me and there is something fundamentally wrong with everyone. When I zig, the rest of the world zags. And when I zag, the world zigs. Naturally, the rest of the world is left wondering why what happened!

If you are invited at 8 p.m., why should anyone not expect you at that time? I am shocked at the cavalier fashion in which guests interpret the reporting time at parties, and also the rather elastic manner in which they interpret the dispersal time.

In fact, leaving a party is not rocket science. All one has to do is: (a) march up to the host or hostess, (b) look him or her in the eye, (c) shake him or her by the hand, (d) say 'thank you!' and (e) leave!

It is as simple as that. And yet, I have seen people tie themselves in knots, trying to make a farewell speech, using superlatives for ordinary food and company, and generally delaying everyone else who is impatient to get home.

It is not just that people have no idea about arrival and departure protocols; they also have no sense of humour! The other day, at the party thrown by the Malhotras, I related a really funny story involving a vacuum cleaner salesman, a camel and a carpet. Oddly, no one seemed to find it funny. Maybe they could not appreciate the comical accent that I used. But my darling had that look which said, 'Shut up!' The 'or else!' is always hurled at me without ever being uttered.

Another day, we attended this party where most of the guests were from my office. After three large ones, I was in my element. I was so enjoying myself that I was about to launch into my famous mimicry of one of our very senior bosses, Mr P. Years ago, he had occupied the same corner office that was now mine. I had been his staff officer and had studied his peculiar mannerisms at close quarters.

'Darling,' said I to my darling, 'do you remember Mr P? I shall show these guys how he handled files in office. It's so, so funny!'

'No, it's not funny!' interrupted my darling. 'Not anymore, it isn't! You have been doing that same imitation for years now. Do you want to know what is funny? The way that young Alok, your staff officer, mimics you! He has the most hilarious routine of the way you pull up your trousers and clear your throat before you start speaking in a meeting.'

I looked askance. My staff officer! Imitating me? Ridiculing my mannerisms! And my darling knows it? That pipsqueak Alok has 'a routine'? This was treachery of the highest order!

I contained my rage then, but all the way home I told my darling what I would do to that twerp the next day.

'And you've obviously been aware of his insolence! Maybe you have been encouraging him too!'

My darling heard me patiently and just when I was about to boil over in righteous anger, she asked, 'And do you think Mr P was not aware of your buffoonery?'

Again, I was tempted to explain to my darling the huge difference between cultured badinage and vulgar impertinence. But because she had used a word as strong as 'buffoonery' for my thespian skills, I thought maybe under the circumstances it might not be appropriate. I held my peace.

My darling and I often see things differently. This includes something as simple as reading plain English. For example, just the other day, my darling and I were returning from a boring party. We returned early because everyone seemed to be depressed.

'Oh what a boring lot they were,' said I. 'I am happy to have left that group behind!'

'Didn't you realize that they were waiting for us to leave?'

'What? No, I did not get any such impression. Those guys were genuinely morose. Is that any way to party? They are a bunch of losers.'

'No,' said my darling. 'The fault is yours. You were not expected to turn up for that party!'

'Why, hellooooo? We were invited, weren't we?' I asked querulously.

'Just because someone invites you to a party, it does not necessarily mean that they want you to come.'

That sounded bizarre to me, even by my darling's standards. And I mustered enough courage to state as much.

'Oh, when will you ever understand,' she said in exasperation. 'Office politics is office politics!'

'Ah ha! I am the guy who goes to office and suddenly you understand more of this office politics thing. Wasn't it written in plain English that we were invited?' I asked.

She remained meaningfully silent. That is her way of conveying extreme displeasure, even when she is in the wrong. But what else can I expect? She is just like everyone else. She and everyone else are weird. They have no idea what parties are all about.

People do not know when to come and when to go. They also do not know what to drink, how much to drink, what to say and what not to say. I could write pages and pages on their inappropriate dressing sense, the reprehensible language they use, and the uncouth manner in which some of them laugh. But I shall refrain from doing so.

Nonetheless, I have a moral responsibility to educate all these unfortunate souls. Starting tomorrow evening, when I have had my three large ones, I am going to get down to writing 'The Perfect Party Primer', which shall be the last word on partying. If people have any sense, it should sell well. But people are weird. Who knows, they might not appreciate a good thing even when it is served to them on a silver platter?

25

A Cool Diwali to All

In these days of cut-throat competition—for goods as well as services—it is difficult to choose a supplier or brand because all offers appear equally attractive. The difference gets known only when the product or the service fails.

Of course, there is another way of making a choice. Everyone would have heard the apocryphal story about the CEO who had to select an assistant from among several candidates, all with similar qualifications. He wasted no time in reading their bios but told his HR chief to hire the best-looking one. I thought the visual appeal criterion was a pretty effective one, so when the wife and I went to buy a fridge a couple of years ago, I thought I would simplify our choices.

We patiently heard the salesman extol the virtues of different brands of refrigerators, their capacities, power consumption and sturdiness. At the end of all the claptrap, the salesman asked, 'So, which one do you want to buy?'

Without batting an eyelid, I said, 'The one with the red flower painted on its door!'

My better half was aghast! She argued that we should consider the brand, the performance of the company, its shareholding pattern and something called its EPS. She asked me if I would like to reconsider my choice.

I know that my wife has no sense of line or form or colour.

But she has a vast but quite useless knowledge of trivial stuff like voltage and cubic feet and warranties and whatnot. So to humour her, I said, 'Well, if you don't like the one with the red flower, what about the one with the pink flower?'

I am a reasonable man and I am always ready to compromise. After all, that is how a happy marriage works.

And so we came to acquire a large fridge with the pink flower on its door, manufactured by the Singsong company. Did I mention earlier that there is little to choose from between brand A and brand B, till something breaks down?

Well, the fridge with the pink flower on its door stopped working a few days back. Nothing wrong with that. All machines break down. Even the best machines require repairs. But what the wife and I were not prepared for was the convoluted journey that we have had to undertake in trying to get the fridge repaired!

Registering the complaint was easy enough. One had to merely wade through slepenteen steps to finally talk to a human being. The human hummed and hawed, doubting whether the fridge that had gone belly up was covered by any warranty and if that model had at all been manufactured by their company.

Ten calls and two hours later, I had extracted a promise that 'someone' would come to attend to our problems.

First came the scout. In hostile territory, he could have been called the 'road opening party'. He did not even try to enter the house, but asked at the door, 'Is this your house?'

For just a moment, I was tempted to say, 'No, it is not. I only came to burgle it.' Instead I confessed, 'Yes.'

'Is this the house where the fridge is not functioning properly?'

'"Not functioning properly" is a quaint way of saying that it has conked out, but yes, this is the house. The fridge has gone kaput. It is busted! It is dead! Come in! Fix it!'

'No, I can't; I only came to confirm the location. A service engineer will visit you shortly.'

My wife and I abandoned our plan to watch a film in the neighbourhood theatre, even though we had been told that it was a rather watchable one. We also felt compelled to polish off almost two litres of ice cream, which would have otherwise melted in the freezer of the dead fridge. Later in the afternoon, we rang up some friends and told them to carry on with the *teen patti* game without us. And why can we not come for the traditional 3-card poker before Diwali? Because we are waiting for the Singsong service engineer, damn it!

My wife and I were both getting on each other's nerves by evening because of effectively being under house arrest the whole day—waiting for Singsong service. We were also kind of pissed off with life in general and also because the stuff in the fridge was beginning to assert its presence, lending a certain ripeness to the air inside the house.

When it started getting dark, we gave up hope of any engineer coming that day. Just as we decided to step out for an evening walk, a Singsong engineer appeared.

This purported engineer condescended to enter the house. He sniffed the air. He sniffed inside the fridge and then behind it. He sniffed on the right side of the fridge and then patted the left side. If he had joined the medical profession, he would have made a killing with his bedside manner alone.

He then saw the plug which had been taken out of the power socket.

'See, this is why it is not working,' he said triumphantly. 'This thing needs to be plugged in!'

'My good man,' said the wife, 'I unplugged it because it was not working. There was no point in keeping those lights blinking if there was no cooling.'

'Ah!' said the good man. 'A service engineer will visit you shortly.'

But I did not let him escape. 'Define shortly!' I barked. 'Is it an hour? A day? Tomorrow? Next week? When?'

'Sir! Shortly,' he said, and escaped.

For dinner we had pea soup, followed by parmesan peas and *matar* curry. The menu was unusual, but the frozen peas and the cheese had already started spoiling.

The next morning, I again negotiated the maze of the toll-free 1-800-800-800 service. I was assured prompt service shortly. The term 'shortly' remained deliciously undefined. A text message soon made it clear that even the Singsong centre did not know how long or short was 'shortly'.

Their message read: 'Dear Customer, your service part 123456789 has been ordered; engineer will revisit in 3–5 days. Engineer Minku has been assigned against your service request. For any support, please call 1-800-Singsong.'

The name Minku did not inspire much confidence. Anyone would expect Minku to be playing with his toy engineering set, rather than handling the big bad fridge which ran on real electricity!

On the positive side, because of my complaint, I had learnt that to the Singsong people 'shortly' meant a time period of anything from three to five days!

The Minku who turned up the next day really had the appearance of what I had imagined a Minku to look like. Short.

Shifty. Ferret-like. In quick sharp movements, he pushed the fridge away from the wall and was lost to view.

A while later, he asked from behind the fridge, 'Could I have a glass of water?'

I gave him a glass of water from the tap.

'Don't you have any cold water?'

'No mister!' I said. 'If I did, I wouldn't have called you.'

'Quite, quite,' he said, almost like an absent-minded professor.

My wife and I withdrew from the kitchen to let the engineer get on with the job of repairing the fridge. But odd tapping noises made me go back and I peeped behind the fridge. The guy was tapping the back panel with a coin.

'Do you have a screwdriver?' he asked sheepishly. I gave him the one that the missus keeps in the kitchen for miscellaneous tasks like tightening the handles on saucepans.

Then he asked for a lemon.

'But didn't you sell us one?' I quipped.

'Eh?' said Minku. I had not expected him to get it and he lived up to my expectations.

I came out of the kitchen and asked my wife if we had any *nimbu*s.

'A lemon? What kind of repairs is he carrying out? Is he going to hang the nimbu with green chillies to ward off the evil eye?'

I took the nimbu to Minku in the kitchen. 'Could you cut it in half please?'

My immediate thought was that the energy-efficient fridges required only half a nimbu for warding off the evil eye! But I was quite mistaken. Minku was only making some nimbu-pani for himself.

'You know, my electrolyte balance gets disturbed easily. I have to drink my salts frequently.'

I was amazed at the versatility of these Singsong engineers. While one had a comforting bedside manner, another was pretty good at self-diagnosis!

That was three days back. As I sit here now, with Diwali just a couple of days away, I realize that in the past few days, we have had a procession of Minkus in our house. They have come in different shapes and sizes, with different parts, different compressors and different tools. But they have not been able to revive the dead patient. They seem to be working to some mysterious drumbeat that compels them to keep talking to their headquarters at the top of their voices.

My wife is convinced that they are incompetent. I keep telling her that voodoo practices differ across cultures and peoples. Maybe we should consult some Korean Juju man.

With the fridge standing in the corner of the kitchen with all its innards ripped out, we have not bought any *mithai* this year for the visitors who come to meet us at Diwali. To those particularly close, we have started giving coupons, redeemable at the nearby Bikanerwala or Aggarwal sweet shops.

But there are difficulties. The dhobi refused to take a coupon, good for two *rasgulla*s. He said he was not so cheap. The postman wanted to know if he could redeem his coupon worth a kilo of laddus for a half kilogram of *barfi*. The Bikanerwala telephoned to say that he suspected someone had presented a bogus coupon. He wanted to further discuss security features in coupons for next year, but I told him I was busy.

It is not just the issue of giving sweets to our dear ones. We too get gifts and hampers with sweets and other eatables.

Both the missus and I are prediabetic, with very assertive sweet tooths! We exercise great self-restraint but at Diwali, we guiltlessly squirrel away the goodies that our friends shower on us. This has to be judiciously done—*chhena* items will stay only till Bhai Dooj; *khoa* sweets, if kept really cold, may last for a week. The dry stuff—things like *petha* and *doda*—can be made to stretch for a fortnight, till Gurpurab. The chocolates can last till Christmas and beyond if kept cool. But for all this meticulously staggered storage, a fridge in working order is a sine qua non!

And there, right before our eyes, the wife and I could see chocolate bars melting away—chocolates that we would have shared after a romantic New Year's Eve dinner!

I lost my patience a short while back and had a long, heated argument with the toll-free 1-800-800-800 human. I know I should not have, but I did use a few dozen of the choicest words that I had picked up here and there.

'Sir, I should remind you that we record these conversations for training purposes. So please mind your language!'

'Well, if the calibre of your engineers is the kind that I have discovered in these past few days, then you really need to battle-inoculate them. My vocabulary is simply not enough! You need someone with a vastly superior vocabulary to train your engineers,' I retorted sharply. 'Your engineers shall surely hear more adult language if this is the level of their competence!'

And because of this conversation, I suspect my fridge shall not be repaired in a hurry.

For this reason, I now wish all my friends a Happy Diwali over telephone. I am afraid I cannot leave home, because one or the other engineer from Singsong might appear to repair the fridge. And because I cannot leave home, I cannot join any of my friends in teen patti. I am certainly sorry I cannot invite them home either or offer them a drink because we have no ice. We have nothing to offer by way of mithai. Damn it, we cannot even offer cold beer in this unseasonably hot weather!

We are in this pretty pickle because I do not listen to my wife. We should not have bought the fridge with the pink flower. We should have really seen all technical aspects—the shareholding patterns and the EPS. And then, and only then, we should have bought the one with the abstract pattern!

26

Jugaad: A Point of View

It is said that 'best is the enemy of good'. But the converse is also true—good is the enemy of best. We could go further and even enunciate that 'good enough' is the enemy of good! Because once we get accustomed to the consolation of good enough, we stop striving for even the good, forget about striving for the best.

This is most starkly demonstrated in our peculiar attitude towards jugaad—we do not just accept it, we eulogize it. In a country riding high on slogans and acronyms, we have conferred a special meaning to jugaad—something pompous like 'Judicious Utilization of Gadgets with Altered and Affordable Designs'. Appropriate axioms might not have been coined yet but we have come to believe that 'good is the better substitute for the best'. Further, we have accepted that *'chalta hai'* is the best substitute for 'good'. Thus, half-baked ideas and imperfect technology are branded as genius!

On one end of the spectrum, jugaad has given the 'Maruta' and the 'Jugaad'—dangerous carts powered by water pumps that ply on roads in rural areas. On the other extreme, jugaad has become an all-pervasive philosophy of patchwork solutions. In fact, jugaad manifests itself in so many ways that we are inured to it. Sometimes we even fail to recognize something as jugaad! How many times have we seen an out-of-order lift with a semi-permanent sign that proudly says 'Out of Order'? Have we all not seen loose wires hanging when these should have been underground; cables strung on branches of trees; cardboard pasted permanently on broken windows and duct tape holding up bumpers of cars? A myriad of applications involve bits and pieces of strings, wires, adhesive tapes, epoxy resin and other quick fixes. Jugaad is a ubiquitous phenomenon to bridge resource gaps and arrive at 'make do' solutions, usually to cut costs.

We have developed a mindset that the streetwise Indian is capable of anything and the 'chalta hai' solutions are the epitome of creativity and innovation. We do not hear words such as 'perfection' or 'standards' or even the more commonplace 'efficiency'. We applaud any innovation as long as it reduces the cost. ASA, DIN, ISO and ISI be damned!

A good example of regressive engineering is my father's Petromax lamp, manufactured by the Primus company of Sweden. My father bought the pressurized kerosene lamp in the mid-1940s. This lamp has a single-piece glass chimney, a gauge to indicate air pressure, a small cup and spirit dispenser to initiate the lighting process, an inbuilt pin to prime the flow of kerosene, and a beautiful blue enamel cover. It also has an insulated handle and a bypass blower which can be used to get the mantle to burn evenly.

In my lifetime, I have seen what jugaad has done to the design of this lamp. The single-piece chimney broke too easily. So as a first step, it was replaced by a cheaper chimney made of thin strips of glass, held in position by wires and a long, narrow piece of tin. In the next step, even this chimney was done away with altogether. The cover was the next to go because it had a largely ornamental role. It only protected careless people from getting burnt and there was no need for it if one were careful. In any case, removing it and putting it back on was such a pain! The gauge for showing pressure was a costly item and it was removed without any apology. The user would know when the pressure was too low because the mantle would glow dimmer. The spirit cup, too, got left out somewhere. And the blower was no longer needed because without the chimney, the user could always blow directly on the mantle to make it glow evenly. The handle was removed because without the cover no one would be so stupid as to lift the lamp and get their hands burnt!

The jugaad story would have ended there. But along came the small jugaad gas cylinder. And now we have the bare-bones jugaad Petromax lamp—a gas-burning mantle at the end of a curved pipe leading from the home-made gas cylinder! You can see it at many wayside markets—the ultimate technological revolution!

It is time we started seeing jugaad in the proper perspective. Innovation should be a process for refining technology and processes, not an excuse for making do with a shoddy product when a better one is available, or to simplify design or abandon safety features in order to reduce costs. Why should we expect—and accept—a good-enough solution instead of the best?

Jugaad may be a necessity under some circumstances. Let us be prepared to reluctantly condone it. But for God's sake, let us not be proud of it! Let us not make a virtue of it!

27

O Tempora! O Mores!

The world is no longer what it used to be. It has changed too much too fast! Or maybe I was asleep for a few years like Ol' Rip. Whatever might be the reason, I find myself being frequently bewildered by the happenings around me.

In a way, the world is not any more different than it used to be. The sun is as hot in summer and the rain is as wet in the rainy season as ever. The hills are as high and the journey of life is as tough as always.

Yet everything has changed.

I recall a time which seems oh-so-long-ago when people were considerate and kind. A bygone era of grace and good manners in which ladies were offered seats in the bus. A time when the aged were respected and the infirm assisted. A time long, long ago when unparliamentary language meant using words that were inappropriate to be uttered within the hallowed walls of Parliament.

But things are different now. People quarrel over parking spaces and, sometimes, even kill over it. Road rage is no longer just expletives and the vehicle itself is used as a weapon to hit and maim. We fail to concede the right of way to anybody, including ambulances. We disregard traffic signals as also the wildly gesticulating policeman. Even a handful of vehicles can create a day-long logjam because not one is willing to concede an inch. Emergency vehicles are routinely blocked.

Have you ever witnessed the crème de la crème of Indian society getting off a long-distance flight? After a 14-hour journey, most are not willing to wait a few minutes more. No! They must elbow their way ahead. That too when everyone knows that regardless of the hurly-burly, one shall have to wait for half an hour or more at the baggage carousel! But get ahead we must, even if it means shoving a friend aside.

Things have come to such a sorry pass that there is more decorum in a fish market than in Parliament. We have become incapable of forming queues or waiting our turn to get into a bus. We fight to board a train and we quarrel even to attract the attention of the bank teller! We have forgotten what it means to be considerate.

We revel in breaking the law. We take pride in being unconventional. We excel in taking shortcuts. Unnecessary aggression has become the norm. Extreme selfishness has replaced selflessness.

Social scientists wonder why we have such a penchant for unruly behaviour. They wonder why we are so rude. They are puzzled by our individual brilliance and our failure to form cohesive teams or societies at the same time. They have no clue, except feeble explanations like parallel processing, solar flares, pneumococcal infections, karma and dharma. None of their explanations make sense. The theory that explains it all completely is my theory—the Theory of Cricket!

Decency in public life has died an unlamented death because of cricket. Big cricket and bigger prize money sounded the death knell for the gentle man in the gentleman's game. And in life.

Just look at the way cricket has changed! In days gone by, it was played by the rules. But there were unwritten rules too. Everyone knew which conduct was acceptable and which was not. Everyone observed the code, and the unwritten rules were more important than the law. You never ran out the batsman at the non-striker's end without a warning. It was simply not done! Fair play demanded that you were magnanimous in victory and gracious in defeat. It was poor form to gloat or grumble. Again, it was something that was 'not done'.

The sense of fair play even made some old-timers consider a Chinaman to be somewhat sneaky and bordering on cheating. Selectively shining different sides of the ball would have undoubtedly qualified as ball tampering! But these days, it is the done thing. And bowlers shamelessly send down *doosara*s and *teesra*s! Earlier, if your bowling action was suspect, you either learnt how to keep wickets or you tried out for the football team. Now the chucker appeals to the International Court of Justice!

In ancient times, a batsman 'walked' if he believed that he had snicked the ball. Now, even after the thickest of edges, the batsman brazenly waits for the third umpire to rule that he is indeed out. He not only hopes that the bowler has overstepped the crease and no-balled, he also does not hesitate to inform the umpire that he is related to a bat—the kind that hangs upside down.

In my heyday, true sportspersons never questioned the will of God or the decision of the umpire. But now, the lack of gentlemanliness has been officially recognized. The rules permit challenging the umpire's decision and it is sanctified by being termed as the DRS!

Test matches used to proceed at a sedate pace, in an almost majestic manner. There was none of this hustle and bustle of the one-day format. That too might have been tolerated, but the Twenty20 has introduced an almost obscene urgency to a dignified game. Of course, we were familiar with the short format which celebrated colourful pyjamas! It was called Festival Cricket! And the fair sex added a quaint charm to the tomfoolery. It was unorthodox to the extent that the ladies were invited to take swipes at slow underarm deliveries.

Barring the buffoonery in Festival Cricket, the olden days had none of the unorthodox behaviour patterns that we see today. If someone was stupid enough to use a reverse grip, he would be reprimanded. Anyone who thought he could fool around like a helicopter deserved to be sent for psychiatric evaluation.

But elegant cover drives have given way to brute lunges at the ball. The finesse of a leg glance has now been replaced by the awkward slog sweep. The late cut is all but forgotten. Wielding a cross bat is no longer a sin! Dirty words—words that were never mentioned in white flannels—have become commonplace. Which gentleman would have uttered, let alone played, a switch hit or a scoop or a ramp? An uppercut in boxing was okay, but in cricket?

It seems that now 'anything goes'. When the world was a gentler place, some of the things that are 'in' today would have invited the most severe, but understated, rebuke. Someone or the other would have muttered 'That's not cricket!' Sledging and other monkey business is now sadly a standard practice. It doesn't really matter who started it, but till a few years back, the justification was that 'they' started it! That excuse is no longer necessary. Off-field sledging is now glorified by calling it mind games!

One captain of the Indian cricket team appeared in an advertisement on television, having words with a bowler. Apparently chewing a particular brand of gum makes him boorish enough to not just hit the bowler for a six but to also badmouth him. Such churlish behaviour would not have been condoned in another age and time.

The yawning chasm between sportsmanship and gamesmanship has been bridged and gamesmanship has been elevated to a virtue. A cricket player's stance is no longer discussed as knowledgeably as his sledging style. Every match is seen as a battle unto death. Rude and selfish behaviour is called 'fire in the belly'. It is more important to win than to be a gentleman!

Now do you see the connection between cricket and the degeneration of society? The validity and universal applicability of my Theory of Cricket is obvious. If we want to improve society, we must start the process by reforming cricket. It is time we took the money out of cricket and put gentlemanliness back into the game. Instead of putting more life into cricket, we should put more cricket into life.

28
Qursee Qa Qissa

My old school has a tradition. Every year, on an appointed date, they invite all alumni to an unbelievably boring programme which lasts for hours and hours. Former head boys are made to sit in a special row of seats. I would not complain too much, except that the seats keep getting narrower with each passing year.

In the 1960s, the seats were comfortable enough. But over the decades, quite mysteriously, the seats have shrunk. And every year, even as the programme proceeds, the seats become more and more uncomfortable. It is not just at these school functions, I encounter the phenomenon of the shrinking seats in conferences, meetings and dining rooms too. It was not always so. There was a time when I could not adequately fill the seat.

I particularly remember one occasion when my seat was too large. In fact, I had never felt so small.

It was in 1966 in the newly refurbished Sheila cinema hall with 70 mm screen. Sitting in my luxurious seat, I had looked at the ticket stub of the cinema hall again and again. I could not believe my eyes! Six rupees and twenty-five paisa? Why, in that amount I could have bought a ticket on the Taj Express all the way from Delhi to Agra!

The cinema tickets for both of us had been purchased by

my friend. We always went Dutch, and I was honour-bound to repay him. The only problem was that I had only five rupees in my pocket, and no prospect of getting any more money for at least a month. In a way, it was my fault. I had pushed my friend into the line with instructions to get tickets, any tickets. We simply had to watch *Lawrence of Arabia*! But how was I to know that he would buy tickets for the dress circle—the first time that such an expensive seating class had been introduced in a cinema hall in India?

The highest-priced ticket in most cinema halls in those times was not more than two rupees. But the refurbished Sheila had introduced a new class with wide reclining seats. Thus it was that I kept glancing at the stub of the ₹6.25 ticket with one eye, and watched I.S. Johar and the Mahdi and Peter O'Toole with the other! I squirmed and squirmed and hoped the large dress-circle seat would swallow me.

It was not the first time that I found I had to fill a seat much larger than I could afford. The chemistry practical lab in college had wooden stools on which some super heavy giant had carelessly left behind the imprint of his behind. Those contoured stools were very uncomfortable to sit on, unless your behind exactly matched the depressions on the stool. One kept squirming and fidgeting but the contours never matched!

E. Sreedharan, the Metro Man, must have loved his chemistry classes and sat for long hours on those wooden stools. Why else would he have adopted the contoured seats for the Delhi Metro? For those who travel in their own Jaguars, let me explain that each bench-like seat of steel in the metro has seven distinct depressions. This is so that the simpletons of Delhi understand that the long seat is meant to accommodate seven posteriors. And no more. But poor Sreedharan Sahib!

He never took into account the eighth simpleton who sidles up, says *'Bhaisahib, zara adjust kar leejeeye...'* and then without further ado, insinuates himself between metro rider (x) and metro rider (x+1). The depressions in the metro really are unforgiving and when you adjust eight in place of seven, the stern ends of all eight are bound to be uncomfortable.

This discomfort, however, is nothing compared to the exquisite agony of attending a day-long conference where you get wedged between two broad-shouldered ladies and also have a leg of the table before or between your knees. It is difficult to sit still and it is difficult to squirm. Any wrong move—a move of any kind for that matter—might give wrong ideas to the lady sitting on this side or that.

I am sure I am not the only one. Others, too, must be battling their own demons when it comes to adjusting derrières in narrow uncomfortable chairs. A substantial expanse is a severe disadvantage while attending long, pointless seminars. The seats are hard and, um, something. I cannot quite find the right word. Inadequate? Insufficient? Constricting? Well, something. As long as you know what I mean.

Bodily discomfort on account of seating arrangements is not limited to meetings and dinner tables. But at least the dentist's chair has a swivelling arm these days. Such a contraption is also useful in the chair cars in some trains. This needs to be made mandatory in all aircraft as well.

Just last month, I visited Goa for a short holiday. After a week of eating and drinking, I boarded the flight to Delhi with a nice, warm feeling. But that sense of well-being evaporated when I eased my bulk into the narrow seat. Had the seat been so uncomfortable on the outward journey? Probably not. The aeroplane seat kept shrinking for the next couple of hours and I started regretting my guzzling and gluttony. When I had to struggle to get out of the seat upon landing in Delhi, I really panicked! I might have even been hustled into some kind of a crash diet, but I was saved in the nick of time! A friend reassured me that the width of economy seats in budget airlines is often less than the width of seats in carriers that charge full economy fare. Really? How cheap! And I do not mean their tickets.

I have discovered that while chair and seat sizes are critical, the cushions too are important. They come in different shapes and densities. Sometimes I feel like Goldilocks—this chair is too hard, that chair is too soft. The only one which is just right belongs to Baby Bear and breaks under my two hundred and odd pounds!

I cannot be accused of being thin. Shapely? Dainty? Svelte? Petite? Yes, I have heard those words too. But I have never allowed any of them to come near my affluent girth. After all, there is no joy in being a couch potato if you have to be an uncomfortable potato. Or worse still, a guilty potato!

But mark my words, I am not fat. I am just so myself. And all that I want in life is to sit undisturbed in my own chair, which has comfortably spaced armrests and a certain personality that agrees with mine. I love it because it is neither too soft, nor too hard. I love it because it is not lumpy and does not sag. But, above all, I love it because it does not contract in winter, and it does not keep shrinking from one year to the next.

29
The Chinwagger Menace

Aeroplanes are good things! They swiftly transport you from point A to point B. There is hardly any lull between the cabin crew making their announcements, the seat-belt sign being switched off, the passengers making a beeline to the lavatory, the food trolleys being stowed, and the fastening of seat-belt sign coming on again for the landing.

Domestic air journeys, therefore, seldom allow any opportunity to that inquisitive blighter sitting next to you to start chatting. On long flights, the best-laid plans of the congenital chinwagger for cross-examining you can be stymied by the judicious use of headphones. You do not have to actually watch anything on the screen or listen to any music; just put the earphones on and take them off only when the flight reaches your destination.

But aeroplanes are also awful things! They keep falling out of the sky! Even if you are so gullible as to believe the statistics about air travel being the safest, remember that a good shaking in a thunderstorm usually scares the daylights out of most passengers. Even the faint thud of the undercarriage being lowered can make the faint-hearted faint.

On the other hand, a train might shake and shiver, moan and groan and give you one *jhatka* after another, yet you still feel safe. Because though the train might stall, shake or shiver, it remains on terra firma. No matter how hard it tries, a train simply cannot fall out of the sky. So I prefer to take a train, any day! From point A to B, from C to D and from Y to Zee.

The only problem is that train journeys take time. And time is all that the congenital chinwagger needs in order to become a pest. And while you are held captive in the train, the pest soon becomes a royal pain. The inquisitive blighter (or Con-Chin, short for congenital chinwagger) starts innocuously enough. 'So, you are going to Bhopal?'

I smile back. It takes superhuman effort not to snap, 'No, I am going to London in this Bhopal Shatabdi!'

After a pause—which does not get sufficient time to become pregnant—the Con-Chin follows up with a few profound observations and asinine questions. They range from 'It is so difficult to have a motion when the train is in motion!' to 'Why do trains always run late?'

Preliminaries over, the Con-Chin starts the interrogation in earnest: Where do you belong to? What is your caste? What is your name? Are you married? How many children do you have? What is your salary?

Why can't people accept you as you are? Why do they need to pigeonhole you into some stereotypical slot? When I face such a fusillade of questions, I remember lessons learnt from all those war comic books that I read in my youth. A prisoner of war does not need to reveal anything other than his rank, name and service number. I adopt a similar heroic stance on trains and never give away more than my seat number, my name and the ten-digit PNR.

Usually this taciturn technique works. Occasionally,

however, I have the misfortune of being cooped up in a coupe with a persistent Con-Chin.

I recently suffered a Con-Chin on an overnight journey from Patna to Delhi. Mine was the lower berth, precluding the possibility of my escaping to the upper one. And the Con-Chin was determined to discover all my blemishes, faults, shortcomings, warts and whatever else the thesaurus might declare to be synonymously appropriate.

The Con-Chin started talking in Patna and, to me, it seemed as if he continued to talk and talk until we reached Delhi the next morning. He totally disregarded my reticence and inquired about my caste, name and native place in several different ways. Not getting any satisfactory answer, he mounted an oblique attack.

'Why isn't *Bhabiji* travelling with you?'

That one threw me off completely. Bhabiji? I mean Bhabiji!! For god's sake!

'Does Bhabiji work or is she merely a housewife?'

Con-Chin was lucky indeed that Bhabiji was not travelling with me. She would have blasted him on two counts—one for daring to call her Bhabiji and, far more of a deadly sin, for using the word 'merely' to describe a homemaker's responsibilities. But I let it pass and hoped that Con-Chin would take a hint and keep quiet. He did not.

'Your suitcase has a name tag of Verma. You must be from Bihar.'

Since no question had been asked, I saw no need to respond. But Con-Chin was unrelenting.

'So, do you belong to Bihar?'

It was a question this time. Much against my natural inclination and better sense, I replied. 'No.'

'Then you must be a Punjabi Verma,' he said, almost accusingly.

Again, I kept quiet because no question had been asked, and therefore no response was necessary.

'So, are you a Punjabi Verma?'

'No.'

He had expected me to clarify or say something in my defence or to offer some kind of an apology for not being a Punjabi Verma, whatever that might be. But I saw no reason to. He continued looking at me expectantly. The sad expectant look reminded me of a Labrador we once had. The poor thing was killed when it was hit by a bus. I am ashamed to admit it, but I almost wished the same fate to the Con-Chin.

A bit later, he said ruminatively, 'That Malayalee chap, that painter. He was a Varma!'

Again, since it was not a question, I saw no reason to say anything. I just prayed that there was no scion of the Travancore family within earshot who might take umbrage at Raja Ravi Varma being referred to in such a casual manner.

Con-chin then launched into a discourse about Deb Burmans of Tripura actually being Vermas and the Verman dynasty of Assam leaving a trail of the Verma surname across the Ahom kingdom. He then counted the number of Vermas that he knew in Bhopal and declared that Vermas seemed to be all over the country.

'And abroad too,' he added. 'Don't you forget the Suryavarmans of Cambodia!'

Starting from Patna, we had by then crossed Arrah and Buxar.

After Buxar came Mughalsarai, and the royal pain kept prattling. Thrice did I ask him to go up to his berth and thrice did I pretend to doze off. And three times two he did not budge. After Mughalsarai there was probably Allahabad, and after Allahabad, there was Fatehpur and Kanpur. And he still did not budge. Instead, he kept chatting—about what, I know not. I was more than half asleep while Con-Chin kept up a running commentary about the places the train passed through and why the town that it was passing through was named so.

I was vaguely aware that Con-Chin was holding forth about Etawah, Shikohabad, Tundla, Aligarh and maybe a few other places.

And finally, much to my relief, Delhi.

I did not bother to say goodbye to my co-passenger, afraid that he might launch on some fresh topic. I simply made good my escape.

Next week, I have to go to Chandigarh. I fear I might again be stuck with some congenital chinwagger, so I think I will drive up in my car.

But what will I do next month, when I have to go to Mumbai?

30

Please to Hold

'Sir, this is Rita from the FBI,' purred the voice in my ear.

'Yes?' I said cautiously. The FBI? The Federal Bureau of Investigation! Why would they telephone me?

'Sir, I am calling from the FBI—the Farzi Bank of India. May I ask which bank credit card do you use?'

I was no longer apprehensive. Now I was just irritated! Very irritated, because when the phone rang, I was just about to doze off after lunch.

'Lady,' said I curtly, 'my credit card is none of your business. Please don't call again.'

But Rita from the FBI was no lady, and over the next one hour, she called three more times, each time demanding to know which bank had the good fortune of issuing a credit card to me. I am not so much shy as taciturn when it comes to speaking with any member of the opposite sex. It is an ingrained habit, a habit which can be appreciated only by someone who has had his education in a 'Boys Only' residential school like I have. Such schooling also makes us ridiculously polite and considerate.

So, I again politely suggested to the disembodied Rita that my credit card was none of her business.

When she called for the fifth time, I was miffed. More

than miffed. 'Will you stop pestering me, girl! Why the heck should I give you details of my credit card?'

'I thought you wouldn't mind telling me. After all many peoples would already be knowing.'

'Would you mind telling me the colour of the bra that you are wearing,' I countered.

'Sir! What kind of question is that! How can you ask me personal questions like that?'

'Why not? I thought you wouldn't mind telling me. After all, many peoples would already be knowing,' I mimicked her, wrong English usage and all.

Bang! She must have banged the phone down with considerable force because my ear had a tingling sensation for a full hour after. But that 'Bang!' also left a wicked smile on my face. So much so that when the missus returned from her kitty party, she asked, 'Why are you grinning like an idiot?'

I didn't really have the heart to tell her the truth. To tell you the truth, I also did not have the guts! I hasten to assure you that I am always more polite than polite and only sometimes lose my cool. But of late, I have started getting pissed off by unknown men and women telephoning me at inconvenient moments to sell me loans, insurance policies and dreams that I do not need.

I call them telemarketeers—the foot soldiers of commerce armed with a telephone—but my computer keeps putting a red squiggly line under the word. The stupid machine says there is no such word. But that is what I call them, so computerji, lump it! Telemarketeers is what they are and telemarketeers is what I shall call them. And all the telemarketeers are a nuisance not just because of their telephone calls but also for their manner of making those calls.

Most of the telemarketeers are devious; the remaining are more devious. The devious ones call you from different numbers each time or merely give a 'missed call'. This compels people with OCD like me to ring back. The more devious ones make you not just ring back but have the gumption of putting you through the labyrinth of an automated answering service!

Yet another trick adopted by the telemarketeers is to use unlisted numbers. My phone displays these as 'caller unknown'. Many people advise me never to accept a call from an unknown number. But of course, I accept all calls from unknown numbers. Why, you ask? *Arre baba*, have you not heard that all phone numbers of the Prime Minister's Office are unlisted? Each time my phone goes tring-tring and the display flashes 'caller unknown', I perk up. Maybe finally the Prime Minister has woken up to the fact that he cannot run this country without my help. But no! It is always Tina or Meena or Veena, sighing in that treacly voice and asking yet again whether I need a loan.

But hope springs eternal in the human breast and I shall keep waiting for that call from the Prime Minister.

Besides their tricks of calling, the telemarketeers irritate because of the servile yet condescending tone they speak in. Even their names aggravate. The callers do not have normal names; they use 'neutral' names. Names such as Anita or Rita. Never do the callers have a surname. In fact, none of the names seem to be real. How come I never get a call from any Atiya Farzana Ashfaq or Elizabeth Barrett Browning or Subhadra Kumari Chauhan? Even a Pinky or a Bubblee or a Guddi would sound believable.

After much suffering at the hands, or rather voices, of the Ritas and the Anitas, I have perfected certain techniques which I am ashamed to admit might go against my nature and upbringing. But so severe has been my suffering that I am rather proud, too, and I share these techniques free of cost and with no strings attached. Use these to your heart's content; they will provide some comic relief and a righteous sense of revenge for those occasions when your perfect siesta is spoilt.

If the Ravi at the other end is selling insurance, ask him if he will insure you for five crores. Casually mention that you have had bypass surgery. Said Ravi will not even wait to say goodbye. Claiming that you are a policeman also leads to immediate withdrawal of any insurance offer. It seems the actuary tables have been updated to include the large number of police casualties every year.

If the Kamla at the other end offers a housing loan at attractive rates, put on a rustic accent and plead, *'Behenji, riksha loan dilwaye do!'* You shall be surprised to find that no bank is willing to provide a loan to someone who puts in hard labour to earn his daily bread by plying a rickshaw. On the other hand, the Ravis and the Kamlas are willing to extend lakhs of rupees in unsecured housing loans to people they have never seen and who, but for their call, would have been enjoying a well-earned siesta.

The most effective response to the guy selling you real estate is to ask whether you can move into the offered flat this very evening, because your *jhuggi* has been leaking more this rainy season.

If the Pooja wants you to change your cell phone service provider from Kiss-n-Tell to Toad-a-Fone, ignore her. Ignore her again. Ignore her yet again. But if she interrupts your siesta one more time, politely suggest to her what she can do to herself, even if it might be a biological impossibility. A more civilized response is to tell her, 'But I am, in fact, speaking to you with a Toad-a-Fone connection!' That should flummox the Pooja for a while. If she is smart enough to recover and say that your contention is not correct, complain that wrong listing of subscribers is a problem of Toad-a-Fone and you shall now avail of the portability offer to switch to Kiss-n-Tell.

Believe me, it works! Every time!

Am I being mean? Of course I am being mean! But when I get the hundredth call in a week from a Pooja or a Kamla, to change from Kiss-n-Tell to Toad-a-Fone, it ceases to be funny.

I am a reasonable man with more than average level of patience. But I do get nasty when provoked. And in my opinion, four calls in quick succession from Rita is provocation enough, even if she might be offering the most attractive terms for purchase of an aircraft carrier.

It is my experience that some of the Ritas stop calling if you adopt the married man routine.

'Sir, this is Rita calling from…'

'Hello darling!' I say in my hearty voice. And then, I add in a stage whisper, 'Has your husband left?'

'Sir, this is Rit…' she persists.

I cut her short. 'My wife is here! How many times must I tell you not to call before ten? Just meet me as usual after midnight.'

Click.

Equally effective is my old-man act. A word of caution though. Pull this gag only if you can inject a quaver in your voice. Some of these lines require practice.

'Oh thank you for calling, *beta,* everyone has gone away,

leaving this old man alone. So, tell me, what will you bring for my dinner...'

Or try, 'What? Speak louder! What? Speak louder, I say! I can't hear you!'

If you want to be creative, include a cough that sounds infectious even over the phone.

I have this rather mild-mannered friend named Atul. He is a real person with a real name: Atul Purnendu Mahaseth. And he constantly counsels me to not get worked up about non-issues such as telemarketeers. He also keeps advising me to get my number DND'ed. Well, I have had my number DND'ed not once or twice but several times. Each time I am assured that the magic will work this time and my preference for 'Do Not Disturb' will be heeded by pesky salespersons and all variety of spam.

It never works.

Atul has also advised me to knock on the doors of TRAI. Well, I have knocked and knocked till the doors were virtually dangling from just one hinge. No effect! The telemarketeers always come back. My friend says I should switch my phone off when I want to take a nap. He says I should never accept a call from any unknown number. He says I should simply ignore unlisted numbers.

It is good advice. It is sage advice. But it is wholly impractical advice.

You see, I am vain enough to think that I might indeed get that call from the PMO, seeking my help in solving the nation's problems. Who knows, POTUS might call to ask me how to deal with Kim Jong Un. It is equally likely that the unfamiliar number is Kim Jong Un himself, phoning to ask me how to deal with the POTUS!

But above all, the reason why I accept and shall continue to accept calls from unlisted or unfamiliar numbers is because I have children. I have relatives. I have friends. And I am vain enough to think that if any of them, anywhere, at any time, need my help, they would telephone me—either from their phones, the numbers of which are already saved, or from any other phone available. I would rather have the aggravation of a hundred calls selling me a house, a better loan repayment plan, an insurance policy or a lemon, than miss that one call when my friends or POTUS telephone me for assistance. Let not the Prime Minister call only to discover that I am not available to help him!

31

Life Goes On

I have visited that place many times, as I am sure you must have too. Not just you and I, but many others have had to go there, be it while treading the path of penury or while descending from the peaks of glory. That small area is neatly tucked away—far from the madding crowd. It would have looked so much nicer if there were rugged elms and yew trees around, but the thorny babools are better than no trees at all.

At the entrance to the cremation ground is that familiar signboard, which you too must have noticed—the one with the words 'Moksha Dham' painted in the most garish colours.

That establishment, on the whole, can hardly be accused of being pretentious. 'Some large platforms, covered by tin sheets' would sum up the structure in a surveyor's notebook. Yet, in its own manner, the place has pretensions, caprices and moods. It sees much drama every day, from the heart-rending to the absurd. It has a lexicon of its own, with the sanitized word 'departed one' replacing the need to use gloomy terms like dead body (used in hospitals), corpse (used in detective novels) or cadaver (tchah! That word is used only in medico-legal textbooks!).

The gaudy colours at the entrance make me wince each time I go there. And lately, I seem to be going there more often and noticing things that I had never noticed earlier. In fact, I was there just the other day and returned much wiser. I had waited with the others for the ambulance to arrive. Please note it is never, never called a 'hearse'! The term is ambulance. Remember that. There was quite a crowd that day. What could I label them as? Not mourners. Not audience. Not observers. Maybe a bit of everything. Maybe they could be best described as an assemblage.

'This is the third funeral in this family that I am attending this year,' said an elderly gentleman to my right.

'So why should that make you look so sad?' asked his companion.

In my opinion, looking sad at that Moksha Dham place was perfectly in order, but the elderly gentleman felt a need to explain.

'We have not been able to invite them even once! There's not been a single death in our family for more than four years,' he said sheepishly.

I said to myself, 'Oh!'

Soon the ambulance arrived, and all was confusion for a few minutes. Then an officious pundit took charge and like the director of a stage production—some divine comedy perhaps?—gave instructions to the family and the assemblage at large. Soon, the departed one was laid out on a low platform, with undefined relatives milling around. I could not help observing the not-so-discreet notice which stated that for the nominal sum of rupees one followed by a few zeroes, the management would gladly provide a floral arrangement for the departed one to lie on, while waiting to be consigned to the flames.

The pundit directed everyone to pay their last respects and helpfully suggested that any money to be offered could be placed at the far end. From that point on, the pundit surreptitiously kept eyeing the pile of money accumulating at the feet of the departed one.

And I said to myself, 'Oh hell!'

Suddenly, from somewhere, there appeared a photographer, armed with a couple of expensive cameras. I have seen many a photographer turn choreographer at weddings, directing the bride and groom how to stand and how to sit, even telling the pundit how loudly to recite the mantras, binding together the groom and bride for eternity or till the photographs fade, whichever is earlier.

But a photographer at the cremation ground? Maybe they have made inroads here too and I had not noticed. I said, 'For gawd's sake, man! You are at a cremation ground, not some ruddy marriage pandal in West Delhi!' But was anyone listening? Maybe I had only said it under my breath because another wannabe-in-the-picture-dude pushed me aside to make sure he was in the next frame. I turned to the gent on my left, to ask whether he had noticed the rude behaviour, but the said gent was too busy, preening for a selfie.

'Oh bloody hell!' was all that I could think of saying.

There was then a hiatus. Apparently, the proceedings were being delayed by the pundit. He had an eye on the small pile of currency notes and certainly expected it to be larger. So he was making a last-ditch effort to get more of the mourners to receive one last blessing from the departed one. Bored as I was, I tried to guesstimate what the pile of currency amounted to, and whether this form of crowdfunding could ensure that the departed one would be able to bribe his way past the pearly gates.

Then I noticed an oafish boy, staring intently at the granddaughter of the departed one! The boy did not seem to be there for any purpose other than to stare at the women, several so distraught that they couldn't care less about either their looks or their clothes.

And then, on some mysterious cue, entered the socialite, making very much the diva's practised entry. With rings on her fingers and bells on her *payal*s, she blew in, trailing yards of muslin and perfume. With a squealing that was a cross between a banshee wail and a chicken screech, she flung her arms around a plump woman, who I presumed was the widow. But wait! I had made a mistake. Or rather the diva had made a mistake, because the matronly figure did not have the foggiest idea who the diva could be. While still in the bear-like embrace of the other woman, the matron raised a quizzical eyebrow towards a younger girl. The younger girl gently pried the diva loose from matron number one and nudged her towards matron number two. It was the right widow this time!

Suddenly, there was a commotion and a self-important-looking gent cleaved a path through the multitude, much like Moses through the Red Sea. He came close to the departed one and did a combination of namaste-salaam and doffing of khadi cap routine to everyone in general and in the direction of the cameraman in particular. One of his minions then brought a large wreath and handed it to him for gently placing at the feet of the departed one. But the wreath slipped and fell to the ground, making a loud clanging noise. Apparently, the wreath had been created by weaving vines and leaves around an old bicycle wheel rim.

The self-important gent and minion retrieved the wreath,

disturbing the sheet covering the departed and scattering the currency notes all over the place.

'O bloody hell!' I said to myself.

There was a look of panic on the pundit's face when he saw the notes fly around. He frantically signalled with his eyes to an acolyte. The acolyte hurriedly insinuated himself between the mourners and the departed one and then further insinuated his hand between the departed one and the cycle rim-cum-wreath so that he could grab the booty lying at the feet of the departed one. His intent was clear—to ensure that the offerings were not scattered by some other clumsy VIP or an errant breeze. It would indeed be unseemly for his guru to be seen chasing currency notes in the wind while the departed one waited to be consigned to the flames.

When the pundit was certain that no one else from the assemblage would offer more money, he proceeded with the ceremonies—largely consisting of instructions for the departed one's son and exhorting him to pay some more *dakshina*. He then supervised the last journey of the departed from the raised platform to the pyre.

While the pundit went about his mumbo jumbo, I observed that in this place of death, there were the most vibrant signs of life, arrogance and conceit. In a place where you would expect 'dust to dust' and 'ashes to ashes' business, I was happy to discover that hubris ruled supreme.

I noticed a marble bench, which would have cost a fair bit of money. But surely, no less than one-tenth of the price must have been paid for engraving the name of the donor! I looked around in wonderment. There were several such benches and shelters to protect the mourners from the sun and a few raised platforms for laying the departed ones. And without fail, each one of these constructions carried their legend to the effect that the bench, step, shelter, wash basin or urinal was paid for by the pious Shri A, B or C in memory of his god-fearing father or grandfather, Shri X, Y or Z. The more recent plaques even carried telephone numbers. I did not bother to jot down any of these because I could not think of any reason on heaven or earth why I might want to call any of the departed ones or their progeny.

Meanwhile, the ceremonies, orchestrated by the pundit, seemed to be progressing swiftly.

'Oh my!' said the tall gentleman next to me, under his breath.

I must have looked puzzled because he nodded his head in the direction of the pyre.

'They bought the deluxe package.'

It still did not make sense to me. The tall gentleman took the trouble to explain that when you brought a departed one to the Moksha Dham, you needed to buy a number of things for the elaborate ceremonies. The price of the package depended on the amount of sandalwood, ghee and other items. Naturally, if you loved the departed one, it did not matter how you would send him off. But if you were expecting a substantial inheritance and taking the trouble to hire a photographer to record the event, you would not want to be seen penny-pinching, would you?

At the solemn moment of lighting the pyre, the pundit discovered that the package, even though it might have been certified to be of the deluxe variety, did not include a match box. It was left to a grandnephew-looking youngster to dig into his pocket and take out a cigarette lighter.

'Ob la dee hell!' I said under my breath.

An aunty-looking matron standing close muttered, 'Oh s**t! He hasn't given up smoking! I don't know how many times I have told him to quit and I don't know how many times he has sworn that he has.'

'Ob la dee hell,' I thought again.

The ceremonies were finally concluded. The pundit announced something, which was not too audible. Everyone trooped out, impatient to return to their humdrum existence.

Some of the assemblage had already whipped out their cell phones to instruct their drivers to bring their cars around, before there was a sudden rush. A company executive-type character shouted at his driver for not already positioning the car near the exit.

'Ob la dee,' I murmured.

I proceeded, along with others, to the row of taps where one is expected to wash one's face and hands. I imitated the others and sprinkled some water on my head too. As I did this, I looked up and noticed a marble slab which declared that these taps were gotten installed by the virtuous Seth M.N.O., in memory of his sainted mother P.Q.R. *Jai Mata Di*!

Both seem to have gained immortality for the price of one marble slab! Not a bad bargain at all. Once again, with feeling—*Jai Mata Di*!

I started to leave, wrapped in my thoughts regarding commercialism and spiritualism, and how the two seem to get on so well together. I was also astonished at the lust for life in this place of death and *moksha,* the release from the cycle of death and rebirth.

Suddenly, I was pushed aside by the oafish boy. He caught up with the granddaughter of the departed one, who was a few steps ahead. I could not hear what the boy said, but the two seemed to be exchanging telephone numbers!

'Ob la dee!' seemed the only appropriate thought.

'Ob-la-dee! Ob-la-da! Life goes on!' I sighed.

32
Wah Ustad, Wah!

I do not know what to call myself, but a name like Alter Witty might be appropriate. You see, I have a serious mental affliction. Whenever I am struck by the neatness or simplicity of a solution, I enter a Walter Mitty-like trance. And it is not necessary that the solutions relate only to big problems.

Why, just last winter I was at this important conference in Washington and I noticed that the nameplate of every speaker was the ordinary printed card, folded in the usual tent shape so that the name was displayed on both sides. But one corner of every name card was pinched into a pleat. I was puzzled why this had been done and quite missed the proceedings of the conference till the lunch hour.

And then it struck me! Of course! The corner had been tweaked in that manner to prevent the folded card from slumping flat on the table! I do not know how many conferences I have attended where the name cards sink to lie flat on the tables like exhausted gladiators. But just fold one corner of the card and voila, the tent stays upright! I was marvelling at this simple and elegant solution when I realized that the Chairman was saying something to me. Apparently, he had already asked me three times to speak. I had missed my turn.

I wonder if it happens to others; but I keep rediscovering the wonders of human genius. Like the first time I saw the word 'AMBULANCE' written as a mirror image on an ambulance, I thought the painter had imbibed a bit too much and placed the stencil the wrong way round. In fact, I complained about this to the paramedic who was in the ambulance. He must have had a lot of experience with patients because he heard me patiently, and with equal patience explained that the reason was that vehicles in front could easily read the word AMBULANCE in their rear-view mirrors. I was flabbergasted! How clever! I would not have thought of that. Ever!

Another day, I was walking along the road when it struck me as odd that sewer manholes and their covers were round in shape. Why not square? Or rectangular? Or even triangular? Okay, maybe not triangular because such covers would be difficult to pack; but a square or rectangular shape would save much in manufacturing and transport costs. The round shape is so inconvenient—difficult to manufacture, awkward to transport! The person who decided on the round shape must indeed have been stupid! Then I saw some municipal workers sliding the heavy cover onto a manhole. Of course! If handled carelessly, a cover of any other shape could fall right in! The guy who thought of making manholes round in shape must have been a genius! As I stood there in the middle of the road, admiring the idea of the round shape, I almost got run over by a bus!

The exact opposite of the round manhole is the ubiquitous SIM card that is inserted in the assigned slot in the cell phone. Had it been square, with no clipped corner, it could have been inserted in seven wrong ways. With one clipped corner, it could still have been inserted in two ways, one obviously wrong. But the rectangular shape with one clipped corner ensures that even the dimmest of dimwits is able to slide the SIM card correctly into its slot. So ingenious!

There are other masterly solutions—small and big—that make me marvel at humankind's artistry. I cannot help but say 'bravo!' when I see the slight angle of a spanner or run my fingers along the imperceptible rim on a shelf that prevents bottles from slipping off. I was wonderstruck when I first saw someone use a paperclip as a bookmark. I could not help but applaud the intricate reflector in the tail lamp of a car. Have you ever paused to admire the convenience of a magnetized screwdriver head? Two-sided sticky tape? Absolutely brilliant!

Just think of the reassurance provided by a split pin that a nut will not come loose, the convenience of Velcro, the ribs on a razor handle for a better grip, the criss-cross lines on a nail-head so that the hammer blow does not slip, that pointy thing in the cap of the ointment tube to pierce the nozzle...!

Simple, elegant solutions! Solutions that I would have never thought of. *Wah Ustaad, Wah!*

33

The Old Is Scared of the Brave New World

Habits of a lifetime are difficult to change, and yet I am trying, and trying, but not with much success! A major part of my seventy-odd years has been spent absorbing information from sources with which I have long been familiar. Newspapers, magazines, newsreels produced by the Films Division of the Government of India, books and the radio—no, let me hasten to correct that. Not the radio, but the All India Radio.

All of these were known sources of information and there was never any reason to distrust what one read, heard or was told. For the sceptic, there was always the BBC on the short-wave radio but the accent and the static often made it difficult to understand what was being said.

Then came the Doordarshan news—unimaginative, monotonous and dull. But oh, so comforting! The fuzzy pictures were in black and white, but they always managed to appear sepia. We did not then appreciate how lucky we were! We saw the faces of the newsreaders and became familiar with them. It was only sometimes that we actually saw the blood and gore they were telling us about. Notwithstanding the visual nature of TV, the news was still heard rather than seen. It remained the age of newsreaders, and there was no great departure from the comfort of All India Radio.

The 'newscasters', the news presenters and the anchors were yet to invade the idiot box. For that matter, television itself was yet to become the idiot box.

At specific times, the Doordarshan newsreaders were welcome guests in our drawing rooms because that is where the television sets used to be kept in those days. Our news bearers—the one with the balding top, the one with a flower in her hair, the one with the childish voice, the one with the sweaty forehead and the one with the heaving bosom—all appeared at fixed times and then faded out, leaving us informed and with the option to switch the telly off or to leave it on for the Chitrahaar, which would follow Krishi Darshan.

The television set itself was switched off after the 11 p.m. news bulletin when Doordarshan said goodnight. The screen would freeze into a test pattern and would start emitting a high-pitched scream. Even if one had dozed off, one knew it was time to switch the TV off and go to bed.

It was an uncomplicated life in which we chose to be informed at our own pace and leisure. The important thing was that we remained informed about happenings in the world.

In due course, we even managed to become familiar with, and then to accept, information flow from that newfangled Newstrack. Every week the news would come, stuffed into a tape in the VHS format, and we got to 'see' the news unfold. It was then that the blood and gore entered our lives! We who used to be immune from violence in Zanzibar, that flood in Xinjiang and that fire in Calgary, were all of a sudden thrown into the maelstrom. We got wet, we got singed, and we were moved like never before! We could see the blood ooze out, feel the earth shake, and smell the cordite.

Ever since then, the experience has only kept getting worse. Sitting in the comfort of our homes, we get shot at, we suffer heatstroke, we starve, and we freeze half to death. Changes over the past two decades have been imperceptible, but they have brought about a paradigm change.

Two major developments that took place were the shifting of the television set to the bedroom and the 'news' channels becoming 24×7 broadcasters. It is clear that now there are more channels than news, and so it has been becoming increasingly difficult for simple-minded people like me to understand what is happening in the world. In fact, I do not even know what is happening in the world!

Because of the paucity of news, many news channels have started staking claim on events and even people and places. Thus it is no longer a storm in Teekop but the exclusive storm of Channel X in Teekop. Mt. Everest would not be there had Channel Y not discovered it! The only comparable concept is the 'ownership' of a boundary hit in a cricket match—*'Aur ye laga BSNL chokkaaaa!!'* One is expected to understand that had BSNL not been there, the batsman could not have hit that four. (And no, I will not use the expression 'batter'. Batter is what you use for making cake!)

The paucity of news encourages the channels to recycle, reuse, regenerate and reprocess the same banal stuff. It is the repackaging that makes the difference. Every happening is breaking news! The viewer is bombarded with many screaming headlines only because the news channel has obtained footage of the event. A flooded hut in Guatemala finds mention but not the flooded city of Guwahati, because no visuals of Guwahati are available, and television, after all, is a visual medium, stupid!

From Breaking News to Faking News is but a short step. Many news channels do not hesitate to use morphed photographs, doctored videos and misleading captions. Alternate sources of news I understand. The term 'alternative news', however, has me stumped. Today's lexicon also includes terms like post-truths, alternate facts, sponsored news and advertorials.

There are other new terms that I do not even pretend to understand. Pray, what is 'paid news'? Or for that matter, a sponsored feature? It is painful, albeit sometimes amusing, to find new usages for commonplace English words. Whoever would have thought 'fifty flashings in five minutes' refers to a succession of news flashes, rather than to some hyperactive weirdo?

The fifty flashings are sometimes accompanied by sound effects and a succession of dazzling captions. Individuals who might be susceptible to epileptic fits need to be careful because the flashing lights and rapidly changing headlines might just trigger a seizure.

It is not uncommon to come across newsreaders rushing through their texts. It reminds me of the statutory warnings of harmful products or the fine print of some particularly shady deal. It really makes little sense. If a channel has to broadcast the news twenty-four hours a day, why try to compress fifty news items into five minutes? Is it so that the remaining fifty-five minutes of the hour can be devoted to commercials?

We oldies are yet to get used to the fact that on any news channel, there are more views than news. All the anchors have an opinion—and they are oh so opinionated! They do not just air their opinion; they assert that you are a fool if you dare to differ.

It saddens me to see acknowledged experts getting snubbed by know-all anchors. I weep for the self-respecting worthies who have ignominies heaped upon them by intellectual pipsqueaks. It pains me to see reasonable arguments being rudely interrupted. And I marvel at the commitment of these participants. Sometimes I wonder what quantum of lucre entices them to enter into slanging matches where victory is determined solely by the decibel level. After all, these experts agree to appear in such programmes being fully aware that it is not a discussion but 'The Big Fight' or something similar. As a rule of thumb, I deem it wiser to switch to another news channel when more than two panellists start yelling at the same time. It is another story that I have to often change commercials on nine other news channels before I discover one not endorsing some product.

In ancient times, Perry Mason was a popular fictional character who, along with his sexy sidekick Della Street, unravelled many crimes in courtroom dénouements. Many in the media, inspired by Mason and Della, believe that their primary task is to be investigative journalists. Their core competence is to teach the NIA, CBI, FBI, CIA, CID, STF and others in the alphabet soup how to do their job. This school of journalism believes it is the finest. But it, too, is bested by members of the judicial/hangmen brigade who scream 'I am judge, I am jury!' and proceed to vilify and condemn individuals, none of whom have any opportunity of defending themselves.

I have held a totally unreasonable and silly belief that the truth is sacred. Hence, in my idiosyncratic manner, I see no good reason why I should believe any news that is purveyed by some channel under captions such as *'Adhi Haqiqat Adha*

Fasana (half fact, half fiction)' or '*Ardhsatya* (half-truths)'. And why should a news channel call its programme '*Sansani!* (the sensational!)'? It is never sensational news but sensationalizing of the humdrum.

I am an oldie. I am uncomfortable with many new ideas—ideas like prurient stuff being purveyed as news with the fig leaf that it is a news story or the airing of the salacious as sharing 'real' crime stories. I yearn for the primitive days when there was no Twitter or X, no Facebook, no social media of any kind and no round-the-clock television. I was really ignorant then. But I do believe I was far better informed about what was happening in the world. So, give me the old, give me the monotonous, give me the insipid and the bland, but give me the news, for God's sake!

34

Three Score Years and Ten

'Happee Budday,' came the shout from outside the house. I got up from my bed slowly and stretched. I winced as the old pain in my back reminded me that I was today all of three score years and ten. I opened the door a crack.

'Happee Budday!' said the saffron-clad figure. With his flowing robes and the overgrowth around the chin and cheeks, he seemed to have walked straight out of some B-grade movie. 'Give Baba a five hundred rupee note and learn your future.'

I was struck by three thoughts almost simultaneously. One, the Baba probably did not read newspapers. After all, the word 'Baba' was hardly a respectable term, given the manner in which some specimens had been behaving. Two, why should I give him five hundred? And three, most intriguing, how did he know it was my birthday today?

The Baba repeated, 'Happee Budday! Won't you invite a Guru into your home? To know the future? To start living anew?'

I was sleepy and confused. That is the only explanation I could offer to the old girl later for letting the Baba in. I also thought that he had mystic powers because he had divined that it was my birthday.

The Baba sat on the divan and drew his feet up. I winced.

My wife always shouts at me for doing that. He looked around the room. 'You have travelled far and wide,' he intoned. I was impressed. The Baba seemed to have magical powers!

My wife later debunked the Baba. 'Anyone can guess as much because of your insistence on displaying the rusted Naga spears from our posting in Kohima, that ugly ostrich egg from your trip to South Africa, and those seashells you lugged all the way back from the Andamans.'

The Baba said, 'So today you shall be reborn! Today shall be your budday!'

What did he mean? Why would it be my birthday today when it was already my birthday today? Was the Baba out to con me?

'Give me five hundred and I shall make you come to life today. You shall feel as if today is your Happee Budday!'

'But today is my birthday! And I don't want to be born again.'

'Give me five hundred and I shall tell you your future,' he said. Now I felt quite certain that the Baba was out to con me.

'But I don't want to know my future,' I said vehemently.

'I am not called the "Happee Budday wale Baba" for nothing. For five hundred rupees, I will ensure that you will not grow old.'

'But I like growing old. I thought that was the very purpose of having a birthday celebration!'

'But you shall grow old and weak,' countered the Baba. 'Give me five hundred and we shall celebrate your Happee Budday. Then it shall be your budday today and you can become young again. I have hundreds of followers who have become young again.'

I marvelled at the gullibility of his followers. And at my own, for letting him enter my house.

'I will make today special for you, and it will feel like a celebration!' said the Baba.

'Every day is special for me,' I countered. 'Why don't we celebrate your happy birthday today and then you can start becoming young again?'

The Baba became angry, or pretended to. 'I shall lay a curse on you!' he declared. 'You shall keep growing older.'

'Well that is fine by me,' I said. 'I am rather good at growing older.'

'And weaker...' He said.

'Yes, and weaker! I am good at that too.'

From threats to enticements to entreaties, the Baba kept changing tack with just one constant refrain. 'Give me five hundred rupees!'

'Give me five hundred and I will make sure you have a happy future,' he said.

'I am sure my future will be happy and I don't need your *pairvi* with the Almighty for that,' I said.

'No one looks forward to their birthday in their old age. I can slow down the passage of time for you.'

'Thank you, Baba, but I rather look forward to all my birthdays. In fact, I always count the days to my next with mounting excitement.'

'You have much to be thankful for, and you must celebrate!' he said.

'Yes, I know I have much to be thankful for,' I said, 'And I shall indeed celebrate. But in the evening, with a nice single malt that I have earmarked for the purpose.'

'Nonetheless, what about regrets?' asked the Baba. 'I can

erase all your regrets. You must have many regrets.'

'No, none,' said I.

'How can that be? You must have some dark secret regrets.'

'And if I had them, I would have kept them only to be shared with you,' I said to myself.

It was only to get him off my back that I recalled a half-forgotten memory.

'Baba, when I was ten years old, I used to be given one anna every day by my older sister to spend in school during the break. With this pocket money, I bought one banana and one samosa every day. Sometimes, I would buy a bottle of soda or an ice cream, both of which cost one whole anna each. One day, exactly sixty years ago today, my sister gave me a *chavanni*—a four anna coin.'

'Ah ha! What did you spend the money on?' asked the Baba.

'Nothing! I ate a samosa and a banana which cost one anna and, in the evening, I returned three annas to my sister.'

'So where does the regret part come in?' asked the Baba, quite mystified.

'Well, it was my tenth birthday that day. My sister said that she had expected me to spend the whole four annas. Just imagine! If I had spent the full four annas, I could have had two bananas, two samosas, one soda and one ice cream!'

I ended lamely, 'Baba, that would have been so, so wonderful! And this is the greatest regret of my life.'

The Baba stared at me, trying to figure out whether I was pulling his leg. Something must have made him believe my story, because with a flourish he waved his fingers in the air and offered me something with his clenched fist. I held out my hand, palm upwards.

Nothing!

'Oh s**t,' said the Baba. Or some equivalent. It was the kind of thing I would say if I had bragged about my fine cigarette lighter and it had failed to light on the first flick.

The Baba went through his mumbo jumbo routine once more and this time three one-rupee coins dropped mysteriously in my open palm.

'These represent the three annas you regret not spending. Spend these and be freed from your regrets!'

'Big deal!' I thought. For buying two samosas, two bananas, one soft drink and an ice cream, I would today need at least a hundred and fifty rupees. And permission from the old girl to eat the samosas so full of oil and cholesterol!

'Now give me five hundred,' he said. I thought the Happee Budday wale Baba was a stuck soundtrack. And he must have thought that I was a complete fool because he expected me to give a crisp 500-rupee note in exchange for three coins dropped from his grubby fist—that too on the second attempt!

'Baba,' I said, 'I thank you for your advice but would you please leave now?'

The Baba had other ideas. He had already invested thirty minutes of his time. To him, I must have seemed to be a promising ATM for withdrawal of five hundred rupees.

'You must give me five hundred. Or serve me lunch!'

'Look Baba,' I said, 'why don't you eat a couple of samosas and bananas and wash it down with a soda and some ice cream?' And I pressed the three one-rupee coins back into his palm. Very gently and very firmly, I guided him towards the door.

After the Baba left, my wife let out a sigh of relief.

'You and your Baba! You had to go on talking and talking.

All your friends have been calling to wish you.'

'Let them wait. First, you tell me what gift have you got for me?' I asked her.

With a smile, the old girl gave me a plateful of the oiliest of hot samosas!

'And what will I get next year? You are aware, aren't you, that there are only 365 days left for my next birthday?'

35
The Night of the Meteors (aka You FO)

Life in government pool houses and *sarkari* quarters and bungalows was uncomplicated. And insipid. One knew who lived next door because of the larger-than-life nameplate. But one never got to meet or even see who the person was. The identity of the loud music player or the grinder of dosa batter usually remained unknown because no one was interested in meeting anyone. There was no point in making friends as one kept shifting from one house to another or from one city to the next.

It was only when I moved into a block of high-rise apartments after retiring from government service that I discovered the charms and constant amusement of community living. I discovered what I had been missing—joy, company, the mixed aromas from several kitchens! Ah! The privileges of living in an apartment!

The Americans would call it an apartment in a condominium. But the Delhi real estate agents call it a flat or simply a BHK, which for the uninitiated means bedroom-hall-kitchen. I moved into one such 3 BHK with a handkerchief of a terrace accessible exclusively to me. Mine was not a penthouse but an apartment with a private terrace. But the real estate agent insisted that it was a pentahouse. No, not a penthouse, but a 'pentahouse'. My very own 'pentahouse'! Something like The Pentagon!

For many like me—who chase the dream of refined living—buying an apartment in one of the 'societies' is the only option. No one knows why such agglomerates of apartments are referred to as societies. There is little interaction that can be called social and social niceties are seldom observed.

In contrast to the sarkari quarters, in the societies one sees one's neighbours, but does not know their names. Residents, who might share the lift with you, stare through you as if you are invisible. And if they acknowledge the presence of others, you can almost hear the grunt of effort that they put in to deviate from their sullen silence. Inevitably, you end up assigning names to the regulars. Every society has the dog lover, the smoker, the cranky uncle, the brats from the ground floor, and that buxom girl who could do with a bit of fashion advice.

But once in a while, something happens which compels the strangers to socialize. An earthquake or fire alarms are guaranteed to make silent neighbours start talking to one another. Threats by the heavens to fall or a scandal are also effective, as I have discovered.

Anyone who has lived in a condo would know that the large number of apartments, statistically, ensures that there will be at least a couple of weirdos and crackpots present in any society. Every society is also large enough to provide sufficient latitude to these oddballs to pursue their own brand of eccentricities or gifted behaviour.

And so it was that I was approached by the man with the birthmark on his forehead. 'Will it be okay if I use your terrace tonight?' he asked.

I was flummoxed! Firstly, I had never been introduced to Gorbachev (yes, I mentally referred to him as Gorbachev because of the birthmark). Secondly, he had accosted me in the lift, in which there were just the two of us, therefore Gorbachev could not be talking to anyone else. Thirdly, I did not know what to make of his statement to 'use my terrace'—whatever the hell for?

Further enquiry revealed that all terraces accessible to residents had been recently locked by the RWA. For the uninitiated, that means the Residents' Welfare Association. The RWA has little to do with the residents or their welfare, but that is another story. Undoubtedly, the locking of all terraces was yet another effort by the RWA office bearers to be officious and overbearing, and to demonstrate the power they wield over common residents. I must have said as much because Gorbachev mumbled something about there being a blue whale on the terrace.

'I don't know what you are talking about. There are no whales on the terrace!' I said. I looked at Gorbachev suspiciously while trying to figure out how to escape should the need arise. I did not want to be cooped up in a lift with some loony!

Yet he persisted. 'No. No. You misunderstand. I meant the blue whale of the game. But let that be. I want to use your terrace for introducing some youngsters to the wonders of astronomy. You must be aware that the Perseids shall be falling tonight?'

I looked uneasily at him. I was new to the ways of community living and did not want to commit any gaffe. Genuinely worried, I asked, 'Am I responsible for the fall of the pear seeds?'

'Ha! Ha! Good one, sir!' he said.

This left me quite perplexed, amazed, bewildered, confounded and confused. If the pear seeds were falling, and I was not to blame, why should I worry?

Gorbachev misread my relief as approval. Even before I could seek any guarantees or think of stipulating any conditions for the temporary use of my terrace, he had assured me that everything would be fine and everyone would clear off before 2 a.m. Everyone? He did not explain the term 'everyone' to me. Nor why my terrace would be infested till the unearthly hour of 2 a.m.

In that lift, somewhere between the fourteenth floor and the ground floor, I had ceded all rights of my terrace to Gorbachev for one night!

As a consequence of this lapse of good judgement, a veritable procession started entering my house around ten at night. It came as a shock! In fact, by evening I had quite forgotten Gorbachev and I had had my aqua pura plus. And a bit more plus. I was looking forward to going to bed early when the first of the visitors arrived. And they stormed my castle, with sundry kids in tow, some barely past the mewling and puking age, which was just as well because I cannot afford to have my faux Persian carpet dry-cleaned every year.

People—some faces were definitely familiar—trooped into my house, strolled across the living room and took the stairs to the terrace. Some peeped into the kitchen, one examined my bookshelf, and one even helped herself to some water from the fridge! They came with folding chairs, popcorn and dhurries! They all seemed fully prepared for the long haul!

'What the hell,' I thought. 'That which can't be cured has to be endured! If you can't beat them, you join them!'

So I too climbed to the terrace—all gung-ho about this celestial miracle which I was told has been occurring since time immemorial, from even before the real estate developers thought of high-rise buildings.

All of us waited impatiently for the heavenly pyrotechnics.

The motley group on my terrace truly represented the full range of flotsam and jetsam that finds shelter in any 'society'. Gorbachev had been able to enthuse many residents to view the Perseids. As far as I could make out, there were at least thirty people on my tiny terrace, most of whom I would not have recognized if we were ever stranded on the same island.

But there were some that I knew. There was that obnoxious boy from the third floor. There was that cute teenager from the sixth. There was that aunty from somewhere who wheezed and gasped whenever she got off the lift. And there was that Madrasi Boy and the Punjabi Girl who never wasted an opportunity to be together, whether it was in the garden or the gym or the swimming pool.

I gave credit to Gorbachev because he seemed to know what he was talking about. He told everyone to watch the northeastern horizon for meteors. We all waited with bated breath. The man with B.O. from the sixth floor insisted that no meteors would be visible because of the cloud cover.

'How do you know?' challenged Pappu, who lived in the flat below ours.

'Because I am a meteorologist,' said the B.O. man. 'I study the weather! And I know that the cumulocirrus cover over our area shall not allow us to see any shooting stars!'

'Shooting stars?' asked Fat Lady. '*Ai ai yo!* Has Rajnikant ji come for shooting some *fillum*?'

'If you are a meteorologist, you should study meteors,

not the weather,' said Pappu.

This profound observation was lost in the hubbub of several voices shouting that they could see a meteor! Beyond the feathery clouds, there was indeed a diffused light which seemed to get brighter by the second. The star seemed to be shooting in slow motion so that we could fully appreciate its celestial nature. Oh, it was a beautiful sight!

'It's a meteor!' said Smoker.

'It's Superman!' said the wag who lived on the tenth floor.

'UFO! UFO!' screamed Fat Boy.

'Mind your language,' said Dog Lover. 'Wash your mouth with soap and water; otherwise, I shall make you FO!'

'It's an aeroplane,' said I as the orb of light passed a break in the clouds. And we could clearly see not just the landing lights but also the extended undercarriage!

So, back to waiting.

Meanwhile, Gorbachev continued to lecture the motley group about cosmic dust and intergalactic space and whatnot. And we kept waiting.

'Which number do you live in?' asked the lady who had with such great familiarity helped herself to water from my fridge. I barely resisted the uncontrollable urge to throw her off my terrace.

So we all waited a bit more. And then we all waited a whole lot more.

Zilch! Nothing! Not even one measly shooting star.

'We shall have much better sightings of the Leonids next year,' offered Gorbachev as consolation.

'Let us wait the whole night,' said Madrasi Boy, with a glint in his eyes.

Suddenly, there was a faint streak on the horizon. There was a collective sigh of satisfaction. A meteor! A meteor, at last!

'I saw a meteorite! I saw a meteorite!' screamed Chubby Cheeks from 407.

'No, not a meteorite! It's a meteor. Didn't you hear Uncle explain just now?' said Sloppy Lady. Possibly the brat's mother.

The heavens then seemed to favour me, and the B.O. man's cumulocirrus turned to cumulonimbus. What started as fat drops soon became a deluge. Everyone ran for cover, down the steps and across my faux Persian. Madrasi Boy and Punjabi Girl came down last, shivering and soaked, but with stars in their eyes!

Their dramatic and drenched entry got many tongues wagging, while several others simply whispered exclamation marks!

Gorbachev announced that the next great cosmic event would be a solar eclipse.

'May we come and watch it from your terrace, uncle?' asked Madrasi Boy.

'That will be during the day, stupid!' said Punjabi Girl.

'But that is so unfair!' muttered Madrasi Boy.

I assessed the damage the next morning. After the maid had swept away all traces of wet shoes and dirt, I was left with my faux Persian, which seemed more in need of dry-cleaning than ever before.

Next time, let come the Leonids, let come the Geminids, and, for all I care, let them all come together! But I shall not relent. I shall be steadfast and true and not succumb to pressure of any kind. I shall never again allow any stargazers to go up on my terrace!

36

The Poignant Cup

'Sugar?' She had tilted her head to the left and raised her eyebrows questioningly.

'One and ten please.'

'Now what does that mean? One spoonful or, don't tell me, eleven!'

'No, I mean one spoonful and ten hundredths. Or 1.1 spoonful, if that is easier to understand.'

'Oh, you science types! You are all so exasperating.'

And that is what we had said to each other when we first met. Of course, there had been others present at that dull affair. As we discovered later, both of us had been dragged along to the party by well-meaning friends.

'Come along, *yaar*, you need to meet more people besides your friends from the old school. You are now in college, you know.'

She and I had left the party early and walked slowly back to the university. The considerable distance to the university was covered much too soon. At her hostel gate, with vital seconds beyond the curfew hour ticking away, she had agreed to meet me again the next day. I had floated back to my hostel on cloud nine.

There followed five carefree years during which we shared our worries, our triumphs and heartbreaks, an occasional tear and much laughter. But, above all, we shared a passion for talking and good tea.

Our hectic schedules, unfortunately, did not have much in common. Hers included English, badminton and basketball. Mine was swimming, tennis and Physics. Nonetheless, we found time to talk and drink tea together. We hung around different college cafes and canteens. We haunted the restaurants and dhabas near the university. We invited ourselves to various tolerant friends' homes, where we would demand good tea.

A few dhaba owners on the outskirts of town might still remember the crazy pair who would arrive on a dilapidated scooter and instead of 'spey-shul chai' insist on brewing their own watery tea.

And never again, not even once, did she ever ask me how much sugar I wanted in my tea. She always got it right, down to the last grain!

We met again recently and quite unexpectedly. Due to heavy fog, all flights had been indefinitely delayed. After checking in, I was strolling in the airport lounge. I think we spotted each other at the same moment. The way her eyes lit up convinced me that I had not changed much. Nor had she. But since our last meeting, more than fifty monsoons must have shed their tears on the tea gardens of Darjeeling.

With neither of our flights likely to leave soon, we decided to settle down in the relatively less crowded restaurant. Without asking her, I ordered tea for two.

'No, no tea for me. Ulcers, you know. I think I'll just have plain water.'

The water for her and tea for me were served soon. She took charge of the tea and poured me a cup. She then tilted her head to the left and raised her eyebrows questioningly: 'Sugar?'

'No, no sugar for me. Diabetes, you know,' I lied.

And then we did not have much to talk about, either.

37

Dodos Die Many Deaths

By the time I grew up, gentlemen had ceased wearing capes, so the question of spreading one over any puddle for milady never came up. But, even then, in the days of my youth, chivalry was not totally dead.

It probably died the day some feminist thought that pulling a chair back to help a lady get seated was an insult to her dignity. But I could be wrong. Chivalry could well have survived that attitude, but it definitely died the day being polite was mistaken for flirting.

I do indeed belong to a time when gentlemen held doors open for ladies. I made the mistake of doing so last week when I was entering a hotel. The dowager entirely mistook the gesture and gave me the brightest smile this side of the Suez. With a lewd wink to boot! I beat a very hasty retreat.

This world has indeed become a nasty place if a lady does not expect to be treated like a lady. But maybe they are not wholly at fault.

That I am indeed ancient was again underlined for me when I got up and offered my seat in the crowded metro to a lady. She must have been in her mid-forties or maybe early fifties. But she took offence and hissed, 'Do I look old to you?' The young Lotharios staring at the girls and almost falling over them were not amused either. 'Uncle ji! Why are you trying to be too smart? You have a seat, so keep sitting!' Worse still, I think I heard one of them snigger, *'Line maar raha hai budha!'*

It was equally embarrassing when I offered my seat to a lady on the bus a few days back. 'I am not that kind of a woman!' she warned. That left me wondering what kind of woman accepted a proffered seat in the bus and what kind did not?

I almost caused an uproar recently at dinner in the club. A friend's wife seated next to me got up, and I thought I would help her by pulling her chair away from the table. But she suddenly changed her mind and sat down again—on empty air! Fortunately, she was not hurt.

Long ago, when we were still in school, a very proper teacher told us that a gentleman should always follow a lady while climbing up the stairs and precede the lady while coming down the stairs. It seemed eminently sensible because in the event of any mishap, the gentleman could be of assistance. I am rather unlucky that I not only remember such injunctions but adhere to them as well. To my sorrow, I had to once accompany a lady political leader and by force of habit, I attempted to precede her down the stairs from her office. The lady took umbrage and would have taken my head off too if she could!

In the old world that I speak of, there were rules even for walking along a corridor or road. It was expected that a gentleman would walk on the exposed side while escorting a damsel, to protect her from dragons and ogres. The gentleman was required to keep his right arm free for drawing his sword, so the lady had to walk on his left. In keeping with this expectation, I always walk on the right, and it is second nature for me to be prepared to shoo away any werewolf or sundry monster if I am with a lady. Once, a friend I was escorting quipped, 'So where is thy sword, Sir Galahad, purest and noblest of knights?' More painful for me, she recounted an instance when a common acquaintance of ours—while walking with her—ducked behind her when a cow suddenly came on the pavement ahead of them!

I did learn the finer points of 'calling on' as part of essential etiquette for an officer and a gentleman. The old protocol required that if a gentleman called on a senior colleague and he knew there was a young lady in the house, a separate visiting card was to be presented for the lady. In all fairness, I must add that the President of the Mess who shared this nugget of wisdom warned us that it was more than likely that the old family retainer who took the cards might not be aware of this practice. Very sensibly, he advised that in such a contingency, we were to say, 'Sorry, *galti se do de diye!*' I made the mistake of proffering a separate card for a young lady just once. And never again. I took back the extra card—explaining without batting an eyelid that I had given two by mistake!

I cannot resist recording here a sense of betrayal. A betrayal by time! I am referring to the victory of the business card over the visiting card. As we all know, the visiting card was a modest affair; it seldom proclaimed anything more than one's name. The business card is a vulgar trumpeting of accomplishments—real, imaginary and manufactured. I bear no grudge against people who need to flaunt their present and past glory, but should anyone get so much text printed that it fills both sides of the card?

It is possible that I resent these business cards because their size is larger than the regulation visiting card. In fact, it is the same size as was used for the printing of ladies' visiting cards in my prehistoric world. But I suspect my intense dislike for these cards is because I have never been an Advisor or Member or Director or whatever else people get printed on these effeminate business cards.

With all my quaint notions and antediluvian ideas, I had been managing to get along pretty well in life. It is only in the last few years that I have been increasingly feeling that I am an alien from some other planet or the victim of some time warp joke. Most of it is my fault, of course. I have not been able to learn the current patterns of behaviour! I have realised I am an anachronism. I am a dodo! A very confused dodo—one that does not know whether to be ashamed or to be proud of being a dodo. So I have resolved never to offer a seat in a bus or the metro to anyone, male or female, firm or infirm, young or old, pregnant or sick. I shall never hold open a door for any lady. I shall not pick up anything that she drops to the floor, intentionally or unintentionally. And never shall I rise when a lady enters the room.

I hereby solemnly pledge to be as uncouth as the rest of the world! And I don't care if Sir Walter Raleigh keeps turning in his grave!

38

Pakad Lega Polis Wala

Within the first fifteen minutes of the train journey, the holy terror pushed past me to the aisle at least ten times. On five occasions, the buxom mother grunted past my knees, alternately pushing her generous bosom or her ample behind in my face. Just once, I managed to quickly get out of my seat and stand in the aisle so that she could squeeze out.

Each time that the mother shouted and screamed at the brat, the brat quieted down for all of five minutes. Then, like a jerk-in-the-box, he would spring up again and run, yodelling down the aisle. I desperately looked around for some vacant seat that I could shift to, but the coach was full. I offered to let the mother take my aisle seat, so that she and her brat could prance down the corridor as many times as they wished to. But the brat let out a howl. Why should his mother give up her window seat?

A short while later, the kid managed to cut his lip when he undid the latch of the heavy folding table and it fell on his face. I did not know which was worse—his yelling or the mother's screaming. I just about managed to get up and move out of the way before the woman shoved her son into the aisle and pushed herself behind him. The kid dripped blood all the way to the toilet at the end of the aisle. Using a paper napkin, I gingerly wiped off the few drops of blood that had fallen on my seat.

The mother and child trooped back shortly, the son temporarily subdued and the mother in full flow, blaming the child, the seat, the railway minister and, for some odd reason, the film actor Shah Rukh Khan for her son's injury!

Quite resigned, I leaned back in my seat and closed my eyes. I wanted to shut out all noise and savour the smooth train ride and the cool air conditioning. You see, I regularly travel from Jaipur to Delhi. But this time I was travelling in the prestigious Shatabdi train, instead of the cattle-class discomfort of some slow train. I wanted to fully savour the comfort of the air-conditioned chair car, even though the ticket for the Shatabdi cost more.

But was I bothered? No! I had retired just a few days back, having turned sixty years of age. Any man is entitled to a forty per cent discount on train tickets on turning sixty, because the railways recognize him as a senior citizen.

But I am entitled to a fifty per cent discount! Why? Because I have earned a couple of medals during my years in the police! A discount of a whopping ten per cent more than what ordinary senior citizens are entitled to! Of course, it is another matter that to obtain this privilege, I could not buy the ticket online and had to go to the railway booking office. I spent more than a hundred rupees on the trip to the railway station and waited for an hour in the queue to buy the ticket. The booking clerk did not know that decorated policemen were eligible for an additional ten per cent off on their tickets, so I had to educate him. I gave him a copy of the circulars of the Ministry of Home affairs, the Railway Ministry and the Railway Board. Then I showed the identity card, which had been so grudgingly issued by the Ministry of Home Affairs. All this while, everyone in the queue behind cursed me for being a cop.

In all, I spent about two hundred rupees and three hours to save about fifty rupees. But so what! Instead of commonplace SRCTZ being written on the ticket as the type of concession, my ticket bore the special letters POLMED! This was sufficient reward for having been decorated with the President's Police Medal for Distinguished Service!

It was the first time that I was enjoying the fruits of my medals, so to speak. Actually, I had been awarded the medals several years ago, but one of the conditions for availing the concessional rail fare was that I should be at least sixty years of age. I had been waiting for years to travel on a half-ticket! The last time I had done so was when I was about ten years of age. I was then tall for my age and I remember my mother made me wear shorts. If I wore trousers like a grown-up, the ticket checker might insist that my age was more than twelve years and I needed a full fare ticket!

This digression is only to share my great sense of achievement of travelling in the Shatabdi train and to underline how much of a mood-spoiler the brat was.

Nonetheless, I was hoping that the ticket checker would come around quickly and demand to know why I was travelling on a ticket that cost less than even what senior citizens paid. Then I would tell him that I had been awarded the President's Medal! To buttress my claim, I was armed with the Ministry of Home Affairs circular, the Railways Ministry circular and the Railway Board circular. And of course, my identity card!

But the anticipation was ruined because even as I waited to impress the ticket checker, the young rascal sitting by my side upended a glass of water in my lap. No one can look dignified, much less claim to be a highly decorated policeman, if he has a large wet stain spreading in the general area of his crotch.

'Behave yourself!' the mother admonished. 'This uncle is *polis*. He gets very angry!'

How could she tell? Was it my haircut? Or was it my smart demeanour? And why do people refer to a policeman as 'polis'?

My disapproval must have shown because the woman suddenly fell silent. A few minutes later, the child was again his fidgety self and jumped up and down on the seat. He even managed to straddle the backrest like a horse and was giddy-yapping at full speed to Delhi. In the bargain, he knocked off the spectacles of a Mahatma Gandhi type of person seated behind us and snatched a packet of biscuits from another child. For a seven-year-old, the squirt had a very healthy appetite.

'Behave now! Otherwise, this polis uncle will send you to jail. The polis always lock up naughty children.'

I frowned in an effort to clearly indicate that I highly disapproved of her trying to frighten a child by maligning the police. The mother totally misunderstood my frown. In a very rapid undertone she said, 'Please uncle, *yoon hi jhooti mooti bol deejiyae na ki aap polis ho!*'

I smiled back sweetly at her and said, 'I see no reason to lie about being a policeman. You see, it so happens that I am indeed a policeman.'

'See! Uncle is polis!' said the mother to the rogue. She added, 'He will beat you and lock you up in jail.'

I remonstrated. The hooligan had made no effort to endear himself, but I was also not willing to have my profession vilified and an innocent psyche scarred for life. Okay, maybe not so innocent. But tender, nonetheless.

'Now look, madam,' said I, 'I am indeed a policeman, but I see no reason why I should lock up your child. There is no doubt that he is unruly and misbehaved, which is a poor reflection on his upbringing. Let him learn to respect parental authority. Do not abdicate your responsibility for convenient...'

This did not go down well with the mother. She cut me short. 'Who said you are a polis-man? You don't look like one. Who would believe you are polis? You don't have a paunch and you don't have a moustache! Why, I have not heard you use even one cuss word, not even when dear Tinku spilt tea on you!'

'Madam, please abandon your stereotyped notions of policemen. We don't need to be the caricatures shown in Bombay movies.'

This did not go down well either.

'Will you or will you not tell him you are polis? But then no one will believe you are a cop. Not even a small kid would be so stupid.'

I looked at her son. Then I looked at her. I smiled meaningfully. I saw no gain in telling her that I had been a cop probably from before the time her mother was scaring her with *'polis wala pakad lega'*. I also saw no reason to give her a few samples of rude words—though I was tempted hugely to use them for her son.

'Humph...polis? Indeed! Crazy old man!'

So now I was tempted to use some rude words for her.

The rest of the journey to Delhi was spent in frosty silence. It seemed to stretch and stretch.

The brat wiped his grubby fingers on my shirt (once), spilt water on his mother (twice) and on me (once more), bawled loudly (almost incessantly), hit me in the eye with a spoon (once), and puked on the nice lady sitting in the row ahead of us. And then he soiled his shorts.

The last was a major disaster because it entailed four separate 'squeeze-pasts' of the mother; the first with the kid, the second to take soap out of her bag, the third to go back to the toilet and the fourth to return to her seat. The kid followed. Without his shorts. But with a strong aroma!

And the ticket checker did not even come around to ask why I was travelling on a concessional ticket costing about fifty rupees less than it should have.

In the last part of the journey, the delinquent son went off to sleep somewhere near Rewari and the mother snored loudly till the train steamed into the Delhi station late at night. All my previous journeys, on a full fare ticket by cattle class in some slow train, had been more comfortable than this Shatabdi journey.

I am of the view that on account of the discomfort I suffered, the Railways owe me a full refund of my concessional ticket. The only problem is that I am not inclined to spend another two hundred rupees in trips to the railway station to claim the refund—all of fifty rupees or so less than a normal senior citizen fare!

I wonder whether the Railway Minister's mother ever scared him with the threat *'pakad lega polis wala!'* Because if she did, I just might get that refund...

39

Do You Have a Problem?

There is a common misconception going around—that communication between a woman and a man improves with time. It is further believed, quite erroneously, that if the said woman and said man are wife and husband, then communication is perfect. Some naively believe that verbal communication itself is rendered superfluous between wife and husband because, with time, they start understanding and complementing each other completely. Even when such mythical couples have not fully switched over to non-verbal communication, they are believed to be in that blissful state in which they complete each other's sentences.

No! By a long stretch, no! The empirical data available with me clearly shows that a newly wedded wife and husband manage to understand each other much better. Of course, they will not fully comprehend what the other is saying, because that would indeed strain one's credulousness. But the newlyweds are able to muddle along fairly well by repeatedly seeking reassurances and reiterating instructions.

'Are you comfortable, dear?'

'Do you love me, my pumpkin?'

'No, sweetheart, I don't like tea that has gone cold.'

'Yes darling, I actually have a headache!'

Believe me, it never gets any better than this. With the accumulating years, communication channels start getting rusty or silted up, or whatever happens to them. This is compellingly brought out by the control sample available to me—the little woman and me.

We are well on the way to our fiftieth, so I know what I am talking about. And I want all newlyweds to benefit from our experience. So, calling the attention of all you newlyweds! Hear ye, hear ye! Listen carefully.

You must understand that exchange of thoughts, which after all is the purpose of communication, is going to get progressively difficult for you both. Be warned that when she talks, the spouse's endearing mannerisms of today shall get reduced to merely cute habits. Gradually, you shall consider the cute habits to be irritating oddities and these will later become rage-inducing quirks.

An everyday happening from the control sample, which I have observed for so many years, will better illustrate the point about the hopelessness of communication between life partners. All these long years, I have tried to prevail upon the better half to share the full dimensions of a problem rather than seeking assistance in tackling the issue according to her perception. Thus a statement to the effect, 'The fused bulb in the kitchen needs replacement,' is more helpful than the question, 'Where is the stool?'

A proper response becomes increasingly difficult with more anniversaries, because the question undergoes subtle changes. 'Where is the stool?' becomes 'Where have you hidden the damn stool?' Or worse: 'Where the hell is the first aid kit? This blood is dripping all over!'

No hard-of-hearing-husband can be expected to divine that

a query relating to the whereabouts of a stool could possibly be related to a bulb needing replacement. Yet, somehow, now I am responsible not only for the bulb getting fused but also for the gash on her leg that she sustained after toppling off the kitchen counter which she clambered on because she could not find the stool!

That is why I keep requesting her, 'Please tell me the problem.'

But no! She will never tell me the problem. I am only asked to provide inputs for some perceived solution which may or may not be the best. Or even viable!

Take for instance her trip to the new mall across town last month. Due to our advancing years and the extremely intimidating traffic, neither of us likes to drive now. Ramkhilawan, who chauffeurs us around, is as rude as the best of Delhi drivers and we feel an odd sense of security because of his uncouth ways. He is a good aggressive driver, and he knows all the roads, lanes and by-lanes. He may not know how to change a tyre, but he knows more abuses than most, even as he has to restrain himself while he is chauffeuring us. And, above all, he loves driving memsahib around because memsahib never tells him to shut up.

To return to the expedition to the new mall across town: a few hours after she left, the wife rang up to ask how she could turn on the GPS on her phone. I froze. I wondered why she wanted to learn about the basic features in her phone, and that too while she was at the mall. You see, she has steadfastly refused to discover the smartness of her phone for the past many years.

Cautiously, I asked, 'What happened?'

'Just tell me how to turn on that map thing which

shows roads and has those funny red and blue lines,' she said. Imperiously!

'Yes, but…'

'Will you tell me or not!'

So, while talking on the phone, I tried to teach her how to turn on seldom-used apps on her phone and locate Google Maps. It was like trying to teach someone how to swim through a correspondence course. Her impatience and my limited capacity to guide her across a screen that I could not see ensured that we were exchanging unpleasantries very soon.

'Just teach me how to go from point A to point B!'

'Okay, okay,' I said. 'Let us start all over again.'

'Look if you don't know how it's done, just say so and we shall save a lot of time!'

'Whaaat?' But there was no one at the other end to hear my yowl of protest.

The bell rang a while later. A very distraught Ramkhilawan was at the door.

'Memsahib is lost!' he blurted out, white as a sheet.

I made him drink some water and generally revived him. From the driver's incoherent narration, I understood in bits and pieces that memsahib had instructed him to park the car and wait near the entrance of the mall so that she did not need to later search for him. She had thereafter gone into the shopping complex. After a couple of hours, Ramkhilawan saw memsahib come out of the mall and get into a taxi. Before he could call out, the cab had sped away.

I was quite perplexed. Where could she have gone? A tryst with a secret lover? Even the thought sounded hilarious! Could she be spying for a foreign power? Again, funny! I briefly wondered if the term 'kidnapping' could be used for a person who was no longer a kid. For this reason, I hesitated to ring the cops. They would quite likely laugh their pants off! It would be a first for them. A seventy-year old, reporting the misplacement of an equally ancient materfamilias!

But I was concerned. Most concerned. Even though we have lived in the same house for the past few decades, my wife has no inkling about the roads in the city or even the neighbourhood. There was a tight knot of worry in the stomach that was threatening to explode like a ball of panic. I do not know how long I remained immobilized with unnamed apprehensions. Fortunately, before I did anything stupid, a cab came up the driveway and my wife flounced out.

'What a horrible driver! He doesn't even know the roads! If people don't know the way, why do they ply cabs? Oh God, I need to pee so badly! Please get rid of him. Just pay him, will you?'

She rushed into the house even before I could ask her why she had hired a taxi when she had taken the car. Obviously, she had forgotten that Ramkhilawan was waiting for her!

I asked the cabbie about the fare and was astounded to hear the amount.

'Sir,' said the cabbie, 'madam gave me the address and the fare would have been less than half had she allowed me to take the route I wanted to. But she forced me to take different roads.'

Of course! If she had told me why she wanted to use the 'map thing' on the phone, I would have reminded her that Ramkhilawan was waiting and that he knew the way home.

Why must she try to solve problems her way rather than tell me what the issue is? Every so often there is no problem, until she tries to 'solve' it.

Then last Friday I got an opportunity to give her a taste of her own medicine. I well knew that she was having tea with her friends, but I telephoned her.

'I say, where do you keep the turmeric?'

'Turmeric? Look, there is no need to cook anything. I have already cooked for the evening.'

'I am not cooking. You know very well I can't! Just tell me where the turmeric is.'

'Are you making a turmeric latte?'

'What the hell is that?'

'Well, it will be good for you. You know, you've been forgetting things a bit lately. Maybe it is the best idea that you've had in a long while. Please make one for me too and put it in the fridge; I shall have it as a frappe. Crème de turmeric frappe sounds nice!'

'For God's sake! I only want to know where the turmeric is!'

'Have you injured yourself? Because if it is an open wound, don't put any of that turmeric! God only knows what all stuff they put in it. If only you would listen and get me certified organic masalas.'

'No darling, I haven't hurt myself. And yes, next time I shall get your organically grown masalas. But will you tell me where you have hidden the bloody turmeric?'

'Why do you think I would hide it anywhere? Why do you need turmeric? Why are you messing about in the kitchen? Why aren't you taking your afternoon nap? Are you sure you are okay?'

Now if I were to ask as many questions when she enquires about the wooden stool, I would get a mouthful.

'No, honey, it's okay. No one is cooking anything and no one wants to have a turmeric latte and no one has cut their finger. Just tell me where you have kept the damn stuff!'

That seemed to be the last straw. She thoroughly lost patience and started quoting me to me!

'Look, if you've got a problem, don't ask me for inputs for your perceived solutions. Tell me the problem. Maybe there is more than one way to suck an egg. Just tell me the effing problem!'

I can tell you that as any couple gets older, their vocabulary becomes more colourful. They also start using more exclamation marks. As a side note, I might add here that in the next stage they start using more question marks instead of exclamation marks. As in 'What?', 'Eh?' and 'Huh?'

But let us get back to the turmeric issue. So I asked her again, all sweetness and light, 'Darling, just tell me where you keep the turmeric. I have been searching for the past half-hour in this kitchen and I can't find the damn stuff.'

'Well, why do you want turmeric?'

'Now that you are asking, I want turmeric to show how it is used as an indicator and turns pink when it touches any alkali. Soap works very well for that, don't you know? And it turns yellow again when it touches acids, for which I have already sliced a lemon.'

'What the hell are you rambling about? Indicator? Soap? Lemon?'

'Well, you never told me that dear Natasha, our granddaughter, would be spending the afternoon with us. Her mother dropped her off here an hour ago and I am trying to keep her amused with simple chemistry experiments.'

'Oh damn! I forgot! Of course, Natasha was to spend the afternoon with us. Damn! Damn! Damn!'

'Language, lady!' I warned. 'Now you know how confused I

get when you don't tell me the problem and only ask something with no reference to any context?'

Anyway, to cut a long story short, I did not get any turmeric. Nor did I get any dinner that night. But I had made my point!

So, listen carefully, all you newlyweds! Be warned that you will always have communication problems. Never ask each other for inputs for solutions according to your perceptions. Tell each other what the effing problem is! The spouse might have a solution for it. And it might be different from what you thought it should be. On the other hand, it may not be a solution at all. But at least you will understand better why sometimes you do not get any dinner or why not a single word gets spoken for days at home.

40
Free Advice

You might have heard that the number of cars in Delhi is more than the number of cars in Mumbai, Kolkata and Chennai combined. Well, that is incorrect. It only seems so because of the atrocious driving habits of people in Delhi. If you often drive in Delhi, then listen to me carefully. I am an expert because I have now been driving for a long time. And I have the experience of more than twenty accidents!

Be aware that drivers in Delhi are extremely rude. Many a times, when I carefully slow my car a bit to send a text message to a friend, the guys behind start honking! I have noticed a similar reprehensible trait among others who gesticulate rudely when I use my cell phone. I just cannot understand it. The phone is mine. The car is mine. So what is their problem?

I must also tell you that there are crazy people out there who stare at me when I light a cigar or flick some ash out of the window. One loony actually shouted at me when I once opened my car door to spit out some paan juice. I could not make out what he said because my car swerved away from his, but it sounded very rude.

There are many careless drivers on the road, so my advice to anyone who is willing to listen is—please be careful! Many drivers do not even know how to use their wing mirrors. Just last week, when I overtook this girl from the left, she was not looking in the mirror. This was just as well because her mirror broke when she hit my bumper. No great loss. She was not using the mirror in any case.

Be warned! Drivers in Delhi are so timid that they are a threat to safe driving. For no reason whatsoever, they slow down if there is a dog ahead. They drive at just seventy or eighty in the fast lane. And they give way to traffic on their right without any warning whatsoever. These same immature drivers brake hard when the traffic light changes to yellow. I have narrowly missed hitting many of them because, like any good driver, I speed up when the light is about to change to red. These cowards also try to make me feel guilty by promptly making way for ambulances. It makes me think that they have not heard of Gabbar Singh—*'Jo dar gaya, woh mar gaya!'*

Driving in Delhi is difficult also because of idiots riding around on scooters and bikes. You see them weaving in and out of traffic, many of them stupidly wearing helmets. How can they hear a horn if they cover their ears like that?

It is the duty of responsible drivers like me to inculcate good driving habits, especially among the youth. Just yesterday, to ensure that the three boys riding on a bike did not injure themselves, I gave a little nudge to their bike when they had stopped at the traffic light. The boy who fell and needed to be hospitalized might have learnt his lesson to never wear a helmet again, which only restricts one's vision and impairs hearing. I am not too certain if the other two learnt anything. Maybe I will educate them some other day.

These days there are many nouveau riche people riding around in expensive cars, and they are such cheapskates! A few weeks back, my car brushed past an ordinary-looking Lamborghini. Maybe I did leave a bit of a scratch, but you would hardly notice it from ten yards away. Yet the owner made such a fuss about it! My advice to any such Johnny-come-lately is that if you cannot afford an expensive car, do not buy one.

Tolerance is another virtue altogether missing among Delhi drivers. I was trying out my new super woofers last month. At high volume, they have a nice solid thrum and make my car really rock like a disco. And do you know what happened? This old fogey at the traffic lights shouted at me! He was so old; he was barely audible above the music. I do not know what he wanted to say but he gave me the finger! Why cannot these old men be more tolerant? Why do they have to resent our youthfulness? Who allows them to drive around?

It struck me later that maybe the old man did not like music. You see, I have a senile neighbour who keeps complaining about the early morning school buses. Many of the bus drivers play the pressure horns like expert musicians. There is one who sends out a cheerful 'prum-prum-paa-paa!' Another blasts a soulful 'paa-paa-pee-pee-paa'. My son's school bus driver plays 'paa-pum-purum-paa-pum-purum!' as soon as the bus enters our street. It gives my son enough warning to rush to the gate. And if he is late, the driver belts out a gay 'paa-rum-paa-paa-pum!' Oh, I love it!

It is just as well that the bus horns are so loud. Why? Because many people on the roads are deaf or blind. One cannot be careful enough. Last Sunday evening, I was driving along our service lane when a car coming from the other side stopped right in the middle of the road. This guy got out and had the gumption to complain that my headlights were blinding him. Well, of course I have to use the high beam—how else would I see his car? Funny people! Their licences should be revoked!

Many people driving around do not even know the rules of the road or the use of signals. One day, on the highway, I was alternately flashing my left and right turn indicator to show that I was undecided about which lane to take. Believe it or not, a woman glared at me as she drove past and shouted something unladylike. Very, very unladylike!

Another important point—you should be very careful of pedestrians. They are deaf and blind and all over the place. Be especially careful near zebra crossings and traffic lights because here they can be quite aggressive. They foolishly believe that they have the right of way. Not only the pedestrians, but others too behave as if they own the road. The other day, when I parked my car by the roadside, this aunty threw a fit. She said my car was blocking her gate. Mind you, I was not parked in her driveway or anything like that. The road did not belong to her, and I told her as much! In fact, she could have squeezed past my car and into her house if she really wanted to!

And it does not end there. There was this rude man who shouted at me for blocking two lanes, when all that I was doing was driving carefully along in the middle of the road!

I think it is time that the traffic police evolved some system—a special sticker or a rooftop light—to identify cars of those that are not to be stopped for alleged traffic violations. In the past month, I must have been stopped at least five times by these dumb cops. Don't they know who I am? I am related to the cousin of the father-in-law of the local MLA! A medium-sized placard above my number plate would have ensured that the cops did not waste time on checking VIPs like me, and instead concentrated on traffic violators.

I could go on and on to belabour the point, but I am sure you understand. So take my advice—drive in Delhi only if you must. But take care!

41

Taxing Times

For many, many years, I believed that in order to earn money, one had to merely sit in an air-conditioned office and drink cups and cups of coffee. To break the tedium, one could also attend meetings, but these were equally boring. I was made to think that if one kept doing this, day after day and week after week, one's bank balance would automatically increase at the end of the month. Empirical data and a discreet slip of paper put up by one of the minions proved this notion to be correct. Of course, once in a while I wondered why the amount added to my bank balance was so meagre. After all, manfully consuming countless cups of coffee and staying awake in those meetings certainly deserved greater compensation.

It is only now, after having superannuated from a salaried job, that I realize how hard one has to really work to earn money. But the harder part is to prevent the money from being grabbed by the income tax department!

In the safe confines of the salary harbour, there were no tempests, no uncharted seas. My financial existence was totally predictable. The same minions who filed away the payslips also made certain that whatever I owed to caesar was rendered unto him from my salary before the balance amount was credited in the bank.

At the end of the year, there were no complicated calculations to be done and no blood was spilt when the income tax return was filed. The salary minus tax which was deposited in my bank account was mine; that which was deducted 'at source' never belonged to me. In keeping with the teachings of the Gita, I never lamented this loss because the loss was illusory. But if one puts money in one's wallet and it is stolen by a pickpocket, then it is painful indeed!

Now that I am retired, I get money from different channels, without tax having been deducted at source. And I resent paying tax because the money goes out after it has come into my wallet. It hurts! By God, it hurts!

Let me confess that now I finally have something which I did not have in my forty years' long career—income from sources other than my salary; an *ooper ki aamdani*! I get money from several sources for a variety of reasons. A token payment for an expert opinion here. A consultancy there. Five thousand rupees honorarium for delivering a lecture. Travel expenses for attending meetings of a think tank. A substantial amount as interest on my retirement gratuity in fixed deposits in the bank. And of course, my pension.

After my retirement, the straightforward task of paying tax and filing a return became a complicated preoccupation. I had started sailing on the rough seas of high finance. To mix a metaphor, I was also lost in the quicksands of income tax laws. And like Abhimanyu of the Mahabharata, I did not know how to disentangle myself from this *chakravyuh*. Terms such as advance tax, cess, surcharge, Form 16, 26AS, TIN and PIN, which I had never heard of earlier, had become my full-time preoccupation.

Then one day, a couple of years back, the little woman

screamed at me in exasperation. 'You were never so busy for forty years, yet you earned more money. Now you are so confused and irritable! Why don't you get yourself an accountant?'

So, I got myself CAji.

CAji? Yes, my chartered accountant. Initially, I referred to him as the CA but now out of respect, I have added the 'ji' and address him as CAji. Let me hasten to add that my CAji should not be confused with the Comptroller and Auditor General of India. I respect the CAG as a constitutional office. But the CAG never helped me earn or save a single rupee!

But my chartered accountant? My CAji? Ah, he is different! He is the person who has held my innocent hand and led me through the labyrinth of income tax laws. It is he who has shown me how to save money by claiming discounts, offsets, expenses, depreciations and deductions which I didn't even know existed. I hold my CAji in high esteem because he has shown me numerous ways in which I can cheat, without breaking the law!

But my first meeting with CAji had not gone too well. While he was suspicious of everything I said, I was convinced that his financial jugglery would land us both in jail. The trust deficit was due to differing perceptions. I firmly told him that the honorarium I got for delivering a lecture was mine and mine alone. There was no reason for me to pay tax on it. After all, I had worked for it. Even the PowerPoint slides had been made by me. What effort had the finance minister put in?

'You might think that five thousand rupees is fair compensation for your pains, but you still must cough up when the *Vitt Mantri* so decrees. Yes, yes, I am aware there was a provision to exempt from tax any honorarium up to five thousand rupees. But that rule, sir, was changed some time in the middle of the last century!'

'You mean to say that even money earned by the sweat of my brow has to be taxed? Next you will say that money received for publication of creative literature is also taxable. I will have you know that I was paid seven hundred rupees for writing a "middle" in a newspaper.'

CAji laughed derisively. 'Which cheapskate newspaper paid you just seven hundred rupees for a "middle"?'

'I shall let them know that your opinion about them is the same as mine,' I solemnly promised. 'At an appropriate time and in a suitable manner,' I added.

'I see that you had two "middles" published; your bank passbook shows two entries of seven hundred each from the same outstation bank.'

'No,' said I. 'The first cheque sent by the newspaper bounced. You will see that the bank levied a penalty of forty rupees. I got only six hundred and sixty rupees for my creative effort. I should be allowed to at least keep this six and sixty as undeclared wealth. A token amount of black money, in a manner of speaking?'

CAji looked at me with pity, as if to say that if I dealt with such cheapskates, chances were that I would not be able to afford his fees.

'No. No. No, sir. You cannot choose to hide part of your income. There is nothing like "a token amount of black money!" And sir, there is no provision, no provision whatsoever to exempt earnings accruing from your so-called creativity.'

I was sure he meant 'so-called earnings', rather than 'so-called creativity', but I let it pass.

'Sir, it is best not to hide any part of your income. Don't forget that Al Capone was never convicted of any of the crimes that he committed; crimes like murder and rape and robbery. But he was put behind bars for evading tax!'

I wondered briefly whether CAji was advising me to pay my taxes or to consider murdering the income tax officer because it was relatively safe to do so.

'You mean I can take out a *supari* for the income tax guy?' I whispered with mock excitement.

CAji merely said, 'How droll!' He was clearly not amused.

CAji peeped sceptically into my fixed deposits; he sniffed suspiciously at the cash withdrawals from my bank account and he wrinkled his nose at my credit card payments. As the inquisition by CAji about my finances progressed, I became increasingly convinced that I would have to pay an additional hefty amount as tax.

But mystifying indeed are the ways of the Lord, as also the income tax department. If they choose to close one door, they miraculously open another. After dashing my hopes of clinging on to my hard-earned honorarium and my creative six and sixty, CAji enquired whether I had a wife. I did not know whether to be shocked or insulted. Of course I am married! And happily so, even if my permanently distraught appearance might create an impression to the contrary.

'Yes, I am married!' I snapped.

'Pardon me for asking, sir, but does your wife have any independent means of income?' I really did not know what this had to do with my income tax problems and I let CAji know as much.

'Well sir, I am only trying to help. You see, if your wife's income is below the income tax limit, we could reduce your taxable income by transferring part of it to her and claiming it as an expense related to income from other sources. We could show it as payment made for secretarial assistance.'

My wife was to be my employee? I had mixed feelings about that! My wife's feelings, however, would not be mixed at all. She would be livid! But the prospect of saving a few thousand rupees was tempting indeed. I was sure the missus would accept the peace offering of a small diamond, purchased from the money which would otherwise go to propitiate the income tax demons.

I told CAji to go ahead and manipulate a payment to my wife to split the tax liability. But in a conspiratorial manner, I made him promise never to reveal to the old girl that her income included any amount received for secretarial services. After all, it is I who writes her cheques, keeps her accounts and maintains her address book. How could she be my secretary when it is my duty to feed telephone numbers into her cell phone and remind her about our social engagements?

CAji continued to dissect my financial status. 'Sir, do you have a car?'

'What do you take me for? A complete pauper? Of course I have a car, and a jolly good one too,' said I.

CAji promptly mollified me. 'No! No! I asked because we can claim fifteen per cent depreciation on our car. So if our car is worth twenty lakhs, we can reduce our income by up to three lakhs!'

'Five lakhs.'

'No, not five lakhs. At fifteen per cent, it will work out to only three lakhs.'

'No, I meant the value of the car. My car isn't worth

twenty lakhs, it is worth five,' said I primly. Somehow, I managed to sound proud and ashamed at the same time.

'Eh? Oh! Five lakhs. Okay. Okay. Even then, fifteen per cent works out to seventy-five thousand. We can safely claim half this amount as expenses on account of our other sources of income.'

What is it with professionals like chartered accountants and lawyers? Why do they say 'we' to their clients as if they are in the mess together with their clients? I have yet to see a chartered accountant offer to pay the penalty imposed on an assessee by the income tax department. And I doubt if any lawyer will ever go to jail for the crimes committed by his client.

So, I let him continue to talk about depreciation of 'our' car, even as he had made it clear that he would not deign to be seen in a car worth just five lakhs.

Though CAji indeed put me through the wringer, he rescued me from the catacombs of the tax laws. He detected income which I did not know I had, and suggested clever loopholes to escape through. When I protested that I wanted to remain an honest taxpayer, CAji reassured me that I was not a dishonest taxpayer. Just a well-informed one! It made me wonder how much of a chasm lay between being an 'honest taxpayer' and being a 'not-dishonest taxpayer'.

My travails make me wonder what all the annual FY–AY brouhaha is all about. The income tax department should concentrate on its core responsibility of generating revenues for the state, rather than waste its time harassing honest citizens like me who try to make ends meet on a fixed income or pension.

My gratuitous advice to the honourable finance minister is to stop fishing in puddles of rainwater. Even the most aggressive bull trawling in these puddles will yield but a few minnows, pensioners and the like. Instead, with your enlarged army of tax collectors, go after the big fish. Yes, there are really big fish out there, just waiting to be netted. Go catch my *dhobi,* who till the other day was charging two rupees to iron one shirt but now demands five! Chase the neighbourhood *paanwallah,* who has a crowd milling around his kiosk from morning till midnight! Unearth the black money accumulated by the *kaamwaali* hired by my wife! She collects wages from about fifty houses, which she manages quite easily by absenting herself on alternate days in every house. And these fat cats would be just for starters.

Dear Vitt Mantri, stop hounding petty pensioners like me. Send forth your multitudinous hordes to collect tax from the big fish. Unleash your Furies and let them strain their artful tax collection devices on those truly worthy of such attention. And may each foray of theirs yield more than loose change! The financial security of this country lies in catching new kinds of fish in uncharted seas. I can be squeezed no further to support your government and its profligate ways. So be gone! Just leave me alone!

42

Olloo The Puttar

It must have been sometime while I was not looking that the frightening new world arrived—a new world designed for nerds and software engineers in which old fogeys like me had no space. They called it the digital world. But I didn't dig it. No siree, I didn't dig it at all!

In this new world, the fact that I was digitally handicapped was brought home to me not just occasionally but repeatedly, day in and day out. And sometimes, at night too. I was regularly proved to be a digital dunce by some things called PINs and OTPs. I always thought that PIN stood for Pain In the Neck, and OTP was the short form of *Olloo The Puttar*—a term I now use for any cocky youngster.

In the frightening new world, I was confronted by the dreaded PIN or the OTP at every turn. I needed one or the other or both for getting a blood test, for permitting a friend to enter my residential complex, for getting my car serviced, for hiring a cab, for receiving a parcel in my own home that was clearly marked for delivery to me, for receiving a pizza that I had ordered and paid for, and even for taking my own money out of my own bank account for my own use!

I found it galling that I needed an OTP for paying my phone bill. Why should the phone company bother to confirm that it was really I who was paying the bill? If someone else wanted to pay my dues, he was most welcome to do so. Why should I have any objections? And why should the phone company object as long as they were getting money? But no! The phone company wanted to be absolutely certain that it was 'Dear Mr 99×××123××' who was paying the bill. My name was certainly not 99×××123××. Yet I was, and am, addressed in this manner quite often. I really fail to understand where the '××' comes from. I have seen the ××× on rum bottles and fully appreciate that. I have also seen the ××× on video films and dare not confess that I fully appreciate that too. But does my name contain any ×s? Not when I last looked at my birth certificate.

It is the same with the income tax guys, except that they address me as AC××××××3× which, if you notice, is a different set of ×s. Earlier I used to think that these blighters' sole objective in life was to somehow make me pay tax equal to or more than my income. But then I knew better. They not only wanted my money, but also wanted to make my life miserable by insisting that I provided them OTPs—for paying tax as well as for submitting a statement that I had paid the tax. This pricey behaviour in the olden days used to be called looking a gift horse in the mouth.

The creature called OTP ambushed me every so often, and sometimes unexpectedly when I had, mistakenly, thought I was on the straight home stretch and that life was uncomplicated. But there it was, the OTP lying in wait, even for stuff like registering a complaint about my fridge. Worse still, sometimes there was not one but two OTPs! The fridge repair company sent two sets of OTPs or PINs or whatever to me, with instructions that I should give one number if I were satisfied with the work and another if I were not. I consider this practice to be bloody sneaky! Furthermore, it was presumptuous on the part of the service company to think that I was incapable of yelling at their mechanics if they rendered less than satisfactory service.

There was a time when the Phoenicians' greatest invention—called money—could buy you anything but no longer, not in this frightening new world! The cable guy, the airline people, the cooking gas company, the online *sabziwallah* as well as his cousin, all demand a digital transfer for which I must use something called a debit card. This is a fairly uncomplicated exercise for the non-digitally handicapped. But for someone like me, it was as difficult as the labours of Hercules and the labours of Hercule Poirot combined. I did not understand how it was humanly possible to squint at the telephone screen, key in the hundreds of digits of the credit card, expiry date and something called the CVV, all in a minute or less without fumbling. With my stubby fingers and shaky hands, I sometimes hit 7 in place of 8, or 1 in place of 4, and sometimes the screen got 'timed out'. Sometimes, I needed to change screens to read some OTP but then I could not find the earlier screen. After several futile attempts, I usually gave up.

I often wondered whether there was any activity or field of human endeavour that might remain immune from the dreaded PINs and OTPs. I got convinced that it was unlikely when I received an invitation to a wedding reception in which the card included an OTP for the driver's dinner.

This ubiquitous nature of the OTPs and PINs made me wonder how my *presswallah* managed. I did not know who helped Ramu Kaka, or his aged uncle in the village. I know Ram Bharose, my night-blind driver, has not renewed his driver's licence in the past ten years because he does not know how to apply online. My maid lived in constant fear of being accused of being an illegal immigrant because she never could apply for an Aadhaar number. I soon realized that I was not the only person terrorized by the OTP and the PIN. There were others too out there, equally if not more grievously suffering.

Then one day, out of a deep sense of empathy, I asked Badar Mian, the cobbler who sits at the crossroads, whether he too was a victim of the OTPs. He gave his crinkly smile and declared that the OTPs had provided employment to his son, Babboo, who he said now ran a cybercafe. Except that Babboo's 'cafe' consisted of nothing more than a small table and stool that he placed on the pavement by his father's side. With a laptop and something called a dongle, the youngster offers a variety of services ranging from updating Aadhaar numbers to renewing driving licences and other complicated manoeuvres which no doubt require an unending procession of OTPs.

In a flash, I solved all my problems! I appointed Babboo my 'OTP adviser'. Babboo and I have worked out a cosy system according to which he is paid a retainer plus a piece rate, without my needing to feed any OTP anywhere. He is happy and I am ecstatic. Now, whenever I need Babboo's expertise, I just lean out of my window and shout OTP (for Olloo The Puttar). And the OTP promptly comes to my apartment and slays all the demons that come swarming after me for OTPs and PINs. Once in a while, I need to go to his 'cybercafe' because his computer and Wi-Fi connection are faster than mine. So, if you find me squatting with the Olloo The Puttar by the roadside—half on the pavement and half off it—do not worry. It is me just filing an income tax return or paying my house tax or ordering a masala dosa or renewing my subscription to some old-fashioned periodical like the Reader's Digest.

43

The Little Woman, the Computer and the Computer Addict

Why deny it? I am in a state of withdrawal! I have all the symptoms: shortness of breath, inaudible mutterings, restlessness and aimlessly wandering around the house. And all because the missus has commandeered the laptop!

The little woman and I share a dilapidated laptop, which for the most part of its life has been sitting on the table in the study. I have used this laptop to learn how to type, how to ctrl-alt-del, and how to consult that sage Google Baba. I spend hours on the computer listening to music, tapping out my 'Collected Works', playing online card games and gazing into the middle distance. Especially gazing into the middle distance.

I have made my wife believe that playing card games makes the typing fingers more supple and surfing for trivia recharges my batteries. I have also convinced her that the perfect cure for creative constipation is to share locker-room humour with my friends via email, and that staring into space is my way of meditating. For her, the bonus is that my retreat to the computer world means I do not enter the kitchen, nor do I get in the way of the *kaamwaali bai,* who cleans our house.

Anybody of even average intellect would have divined that the tacit understanding has always been that the laptop belongs equally to both of us, as long as I have exclusive usage rights. This eminently sensible arrangement has now been disrupted! My wife's kitty club plans to publish an in-house journal. For some mysterious reason, they have decided that my dear wife is best suited to type out all their proceedings and whatever literary offerings that might be made by members of the club. And thus I am denied access to the laptop. Oh my solitaire! My surfing! My chats! My lovely ghazals! I can do nothing at all without access to the computer!

There is a substantial amount of medical literature available regarding the dependence of the millennials on their smartphones. Regrettably, there is hardly anything that Google Baba has to say about the addiction of the older generation to the laptop. Oldies with failing eyesight need the large keyboard, which only a laptop can provide. With a lot of difficulty, I have learnt how to type using more than just the index finger. By monopolizing the computer, my wife is now forcing me to use the phone for checking my mail and consulting Google ji. I am constrained to use my thumbs for typing. And I am all thumbs when it comes to using all thumbs!

I tried to assert my laptop usage rights but the campaign was a non-starter. I then suggested a complicated time-share programme to the missus which she rejected with a summary shake of the head. I have pleaded for even a few minutes to use the computer every morning, but the little woman's kitty club journal always takes precedence. And her journal seems to be never-ending! This is partly because she is slower than even I am at typing and partly because the manuscripts are more voluminous than Manusmriti. And equally indecipherable! She can hardly make out the spidery handwritings. So last week I deviously offered to type the journal for her. But she saw through that stratagem.

'Don't you dare touch the computer as long as I need to use it! Just your touch might make the computer crash or ruin the file!'

To ensure there was no inadvertent disaster, I asked her the name of her file. 'Don't you know? I am typing kitty club matter under the filename "All Ladies of the Club".'

'So, if a computer file is ruined, is it said to be de-filed?' I asked with my most innocent face. 'Because if that be so, would I be able to claim to have de-filed "All Ladies of the Club"?'

The historian of the club looked at me with disdain, 'A computer file is said to be corrupted, not de-filed.'

Even as I had the passing thought that she could be taking tuitions in computer science, I was thrown off-balance. But only momentarily!

'I see,' said I. 'If my mere touch makes the computer crash or corrupts your file, I would not be lying if I said that I corrupted "All Ladies of the Club"?'

That did not go down too well either and my wife assured me that I would be lying in my grave if I made any such claim.

'Here lies XYZ—he corrupted "All Ladies of the Club"!' Not a bad epitaph, that!

And so the days have passed. Meanwhile, I have made no progress on my autobiography. 'My Compleat Works' are in limbo and 'The Great Novel' has hit the pause button. I am also suffering pangs of separation. It is as if my blankie has been snatched away. My pacifier! I am in withdrawal! I am having fully-fledged delirium tremens or something close. My nose tip is often cold, my eyes are watery and my fingertips are itchy. I am reduced to being a gibbering idiot, pining to touch the beloved laptop but denied access. Not even a fleeting caress!

Yesterday, I felt that it would be some balm to my tormented soul if I were to listen to the media player.

'I say, put some music on at least,' I said to the dedicated Hansard as she sat at the computer.

But she would have none of it. 'It is so distracting!' she declared. 'I can't concentrate if this thing keeps playing your depressing music from under my fingertips.'

'Okay,' said I, 'then please put on some lively music—the kind you like.'

'I like silence,' was the curt response of the chronicler of the kitty club.

Can anyone blame me if I am severely disoriented? I am not the only disoriented one. Even the kaamwaali bai, aka KB, does not know how to react to a spectre floating around like the ghost of Banquo. Like Banquo, I too am the restless one. I keep flitting from room to room, aimlessly picking up a book here and flicking some imaginary dust there. I frequently obstruct KB's rapid progress down the corridor; I get underfoot while KB advances up the staircase. And once KB almost swept me out of the house with the rest of the dirt!

So here I am. Putting pen on paper after God knows how many years. Reading the newspaper to find out what is happening in the world. Shuffling a (hard copy) pack of cards to play a game of Patience. The most irksome thing is the fact that I have to make telephone calls instead of sending emails. All my computer-savvy friends are left wondering whether I have finally lost it.

I do not know how long I can bear the strain of being away from the laptop. The little woman seems to have stumbled onto the fact that the study is the most peaceful part of the house. She has perfected that stance of sitting at the computer so that she can look out of the window, while appearing to be busy at the same time. Now I just hope she does not discover the joys of gazing into the middle distance; otherwise, I shall never be able to reclaim the laptop.

44

The Best Advice I Ever Got

I was somewhat taken aback when that young student asked me, 'Sir, what is the best advice that you have ever received?'

I have weathered many a storm in the past sixty-odd years. I have fought my share of battles—within the boardroom and without—and come out better than most. I have conquered the molehills and mountains. I have been feted and acclaimed. And I have been generous with my advice and handed them out—here, there and everywhere. The advice was sought in a few cases but in many cases, even when it was not sought, it had been sorely needed. I have lost count of the number of people who must have benefited from my wise counsel.

But when did I receive any advice? And the best advice? This question stopped me dead in my tracks. I had been in full flow, basking in the glow of being the honoured guest and the font of all wisdom.

I must explain that this question was put to me at the concluding session of a day-long seminar on 'The Importance of Mentors', where I was the star speaker and had been given the floor for a whole hour. The structured talk to students of the business school had gone well and we were at the end of the Q&A. I was thoroughly enjoying it! The hall was large, the audience was attentive, the air conditioning was effective, and the sound system was excellent. Two or three spotlights were focussed on me, and I was certain that in my dark suit and dazzling white shirt, I was an impressive figure.

To add to my joy was the fact that the lectern was a modern affair, made of transparent acrylic. I hate those bulky wooden things that hide the speaker completely. As you know, I am rather short and when I stand behind a wooden lectern, the audience can see nothing except my disembodied head on the tabletop. I was sure that here the audience could see me, from the slicked-back grey hair to the shiny oxfords.

'So! Umm... What is the best bit of advice that I have ever been given? Good question, that,' said I, playing for time. 'Why is it that people are more willing to give advice than to accept it? And even if someone listens to the advice, why does he or she find it so difficult to act on it?'

I dallied for a while more by making profound observations about the different kinds of advice, all the while desperately trying to remember whether I had ever been given any advice by anybody.

I could recall umpteen instances when I had helped others, but for the life of me I could not recall anyone ever having given me any advice. I thought hard. Nope. Not a single instance. I stopped talking.

Silence.

Then just as the hiatus was about to become embarrassing, I recalled one instance from long ago. It was also a deliciously naughty anecdote which I thought would go down well with this mixed group of young adults. So I let the silence drag on a bit more for dramatic effect and then launched into a short story.

'Well, you know,' I said. 'It was a long time ago, but I

do recall an eminently sensible piece of advice that I got from the football coach in my school. It was very good advice that I have never forgotten.'

I knew my audience was all ears by the way many of them eagerly leaned forward in their seats. You could slice the silence in the hall with a knife.

'You see, when I was about nine years of age, my football coach said to our group of footballers, "Always make sure your fly is buttoned up!" In those days, men's shorts and trousers did not have zippers. The fly was closed with three or four buttons. You had to undo the buttons and close them again when you were done.

'All of us young boys were briefly wonder-struck by these profound words. We nodded our heads sagely. "Always check that your fly is buttoned," we repeated. And then one of us, I forget who, asked cheekily, "Coach, why do you say we must always make sure that our fly is buttoned up?"

'The coach said, "Because an open fly gets you into all kinds of trouble!"

'He went on to narrate an incident from his childhood when he was about ten years old. He recounted a moment during a football game when he got an easy opportunity of scoring a goal. He had taken a high pass, leaving the full backs stranded near the middle of the field and managed to dribble past the goalkeeper. According to the coach, he was just outside the penalty arc with the ball under control. The wide-open goal was right in front of him and all that he needed to do was to nudge the ball in the right direction and into the net. Even as he was exulting that he would score the winning goal, there was a slight mishap. You see, he was not wearing any underpants and his fly was open! Consequently, as he struggled to close the buttons on the errant bit of anatomy, the football rolled away to the side and he missed a sitter of a goal.

"'So boys!' said our coach, "Always make sure that your fly is closed."'

I concluded by repeating, 'Always make sure that your fly is zipped! And that is the best advice I ever got.'

There was thunderous applause as I ended the Q&A on this note. I knew that my talk and handling of the questions had indeed been superlative. But the clapping seemed quite disproportionate and one or two catcalls seemed inappropriate. I must admit, I was a bit flustered and embarrassed by the ovation.

Nonetheless, I took a bow and then, very graciously, I bowed low once more. The second bow was a grand gesture that would have made any Shakespearean actor proud! It was then that I realized why the audience had reacted so enthusiastically to my anecdote about the best advice I ever received, and why the world would be a better place if only people acted on the advice given to them. For as I bowed low, I saw that my own fly was open, and a small part of my white shirt was sticking out. It struck me then that this bit of dazzling white must have been visible to all for the best part of an hour as I stood under the spotlights behind the transparent lectern!

I doubt if I shall feel up to accepting an invitation to mentor youngsters in that place again.

45

The Love Song of King Uncle

His name was Rajah.
God knows with what hopes his parents had named him so. But to us, the assorted cousins of a dysfunctional extended family, it was an incongruous name because there was nothing even remotely regal about him.

He was short and balding, with perpetually drooping shoulders and a straggly moustache. The only notable achievement in his life was that he fell in love with, and married, a girl called Queenie. Since the girl called Queenie happened to be our aunt, it was only natural that he came to be referred to as 'King Uncle' by everyone in the family—nephews and nieces, uncles and aunts, servants and maids.

The King–Queenie romance had taken place much before I was born, but I knew the love story well. After all, gossip within families passes on very efficiently from one cousin to the other and from one generation to the next, accompanied with titters and sniggers!

Has anyone ever advanced the hypothesis that perfectly matched couples—the victims of Cupid—reach a neutral state of resentful coexistence after a period of time? The corollary being that perfectly ill-matched couples—the victims of arranged marriages—also reach the same state of resentful coexistence in approximately the same time.

King Uncle and Aunt Queenie provided the perfect empirical evidence in support of any such hypothesis. They had started as sweethearts and had had a traditional wedding with all the trappings of an arranged marriage. It was difficult to decide whether it was a love marriage or an arranged marriage. But no matter how one categorized their union, their reaching a state of resentful coexistence was a foregone conclusion. The only imponderable had probably been, 'How soon?'

They must have reached the state of detente fairly early because I never saw them in any state other than constant domestic disharmony. They seemed to be held together by those hoops of steel called children—first a daughter, then a son, then a set of twins (both girls) and then a boy again—because their marriage seemed to be loveless. Even in that lovelessness, however, both seemed supremely happy.

We marvelled at their equanimity and ordinariness. There was little for them to be excited about or to look forward to. But King Uncle and Aunt Queenie were not even aware how humdrum was the life that they led. No excitement, no distractions, no uncertainties. Not once was either of them heard declaring their love for the other and never did we witness any display of affection. Inexplicably, they seemed contented!

We sometimes pitied them because we thought that they did not even know enough to be unhappy. They were an odd couple indeed, with little understanding of each other. They almost always talked at cross-purposes, and it was only sometimes that we could see any interrelation in their elliptical exchanges. Sometimes there seemed to be some underlying stream of consciousness that both might have been aware of; but, to the casual observer, their words spoken at each other never seemed to indicate any shared thought or idea.

Their desultory discussions were the source of much merriment among us, the children. Out of earshot of Aunt Queenie, we would mimic their conversations and double over with laughter.

The most amusing of their exchanges, with appropriate pauses, usually related to King Uncle and his club:

He: I had a tough day in the office. I am going to the club!
[No pause at all]
She: Why must you go the club? There is nothing there but your good-for-nothing friends who smoke and drink, drink and smoke!
[Long uncomfortable pause]
He: I will definitely go today, but I think I should not go so often.
[Short pause]
She: But what will you do at home?
[Shorter pause]
He: Maybe I shouldn't go today. My friends only drink and smoke.
[Long ruminative pause]
She: If a man sits at home, he only gets depressed.
[Tense pause]
He: No, I will definitely not go to the club.
[No pause]
She: You must go! After all, a man must have friends. And a bit of liquor is good for your health!
[Pregnant pause]
He: It is decided then. I will terminate my club membership.
[Hostile pause]

She: I insist! If you won't go, there will be no one worse than me.

The threat 'There will be no one worse than me,' hurled with the correct measure of vehemence, was the ultimate gambit and it was guaranteed to push King Uncle to the club. Or to his office. Or to the market. Or up on to a rickety stool to change a light bulb.

This gambit—'Queenie's Gambit', to coin a phrase—was used several times a day, from King Uncle not eating his veggies or putting additional salt on his dal, to driving too fast. It was pure nag, nag and nag, with no restraint or respite.

The years passed. I grew older and left home for higher studies. As so often happens in large extended families, I lost track of our Aunt Queenie and King Uncle with the passage of time.

A few years later, at the wedding of a distant cousin's son, I learnt that Aunt Queenie had finally stopped nagging King Uncle. Again, it was at some similar family function a couple of years later that I learnt that King Uncle too had decided to go upstairs. Someone said that he died soon after his wife because he could not bear to live without her nagging.

Though King Uncle and Aunt Queenie left for the hereafter, their memory and the memory of their idiosyncrasies remained. Whenever I met my cousins, we recalled this story or that. We mimicked their interminable arguments and we laughed. We especially reminisced about their 'Going to the Club' routine and would soon be ROFL, as they say these days.

After we got married, my wife soon realized that, within the family, King Uncle and Aunt Queenie were some kind of a private code for describing amusing marital discord situations.

She insisted on being included in the charmed circle and I had to narrate the love song of King Uncle to my sweetheart.

I should mention here that like Aunt Queenie and King Uncle, my sweetheart and I too had a love-arranged marriage. But our similarity with Aunt Queenie–King Uncle's unremarkable life and humdrum existence ends there. I am tall, dark and handsome. Far from being bald, my mane of silver-grey hair is the envy of my friends. My wife remains a petite and pretty woman, unlike the frumpy Aunt Queenie. In our marriage, the magic has persisted for the past forty years, without needing the cement of several children. In fact, my wife and I get on so well that very often the two of us sit for hours without exchanging a word. And yet we are in communion with each other.

I do not remember the last time the little woman said 'I love you' to me. She does not need to tell me that she loves me, because she says it in different ways many times a day.

She starts worrying if I so much as cough or even belch loudly. She reminds me to take the medicine for my blood pressure every morning and before going to bed. She warns me against driving fast. She never allows me to drink more than two pegs and if she sees me so much as look at a samosa, she swoops on me like a hawk. At night, if I get up to drink water, she wakes up too.

I know she does all this because she loves me so much.

Of course, once in a while my wife objects to my going to play golf. I readily agree to abandon all plans till she suggests that it would be good for me to go out and get some exercise. I agree that exercise is good but I must also spend time with her. It is at this stage that she declares that I must meet my friends too. And when I vehemently refuse to go, she says I had better go or else there shall be no one worse than her. We both know that she is using Queenie's gambit just to underline our lovey-dovey situation.

Yesterday, the little woman and I again went through the charade of going or not going for golf. Ultimately, she pushed me out of our apartment. While I was waiting for the lift, she kept chatting.

'Don't overstrain yourself!' she said.

'Drive carefully!' she instructed.

'Call when you reach the club!' she directed.

As I entered the lift, I glanced at my reflection in the large mirror. Though I do not have his sagging shoulders or a balding head, for just a fleeting moment I seemed to be the spitting image of King Uncle! But it must have been some trick of the light or the slight vibration of the lift. After all, King Uncle and I are so dissimilar!